Other Books by Katherine Hetzel

StarMark
Kingstone
Squidge's Guide to Super Stories

The Chronicles of Issraya

Book 1: Tilda of Merjan
Book 2: Tilda and the Mines of Pergatt
Book 3: Tilda and the Bones of Kradlock
Book 4: Tilda and the Dragons of Nargan

HOLLOW DAUGHTER

To Alison —
With love,
Katherine
x.

HOLLOW DAUGHTER

a collection of short stories by
KATHERINE HETZEL

GusGus Press • Bedazzled Ink Publishing
Fairfield, California

© 2023 Katherine Hetzel

All rights reserved. No part of this publication may be reproduced or transmitted in any means, electronic or mechanical, without permission in writing from the publisher.

978-1-960373-16-8 paperback

Cover Design
by
Stevie Ashurst

"Washing Day," *Leicester Writes Short Story Prize Anthology*, 2020
"Potato Soup," *Stories for Homes Online Anthology*, 2017
"The Pink Feather Boa Incident," *Leicester Writes Short Story Prize Anthology*, 2017
"The Colour of Life," *The Colour of Life and other stories*, Retreat West Short Story Competition Anthology, 2013
"Homeland," *Stories for Homes*, Vol 1, 2013
"Cirque de la Vie," online at retreatwest.co.uk/winners-circus-flash, 2021
"Miss Aveline's Summerhouse," *Leicester Writes Short Story Prize Anthology*, 2021
"One Cold Coin," From *Bloom to Blizzard Charity Anthology*, WI4C Leicester, 2020
"Thread," *A Seeming Glass: A Collection of Reflected Tales*, The Random Writers, 2014

GusGus Press
a division of
Bedazzled Ink Publishing Company
Fairfield, California
http://www.bedazzledink.com

Acknowledgements

Thanks go to:
 Athelstone and AlanP, who set the best peer-judged short story competitions.
 Rulers Wit, for offering the prize of a book cover design.
 Stevie Ashurst, for designing a beautiful cover with the deepest of hollows.
 The team at Bedazzled Ink for giving my more "grown up" writing a chance.

Introduction

I write a lot of fantasy about women. And girls.

About when they are in control and when they have no control. About when they are involved in imagined rituals of their own or others' making. About their immersion in both ordinary and extraordinary situations.

Some of these short stories and flash fiction pieces were written specifically for competitions, others simply because inspiration struck. Several have been published in anthologies and are republished here, others have been tweaked a little since their original appearance on my blog, and others have been written especially for this collection.

I hope that readers will find in these pages something which resonates with their own lived or imagined experience of being female.

Hollow Daughter

The knock on her door pulled Alish out of her doze with a start. "What in all the Saints—?" She straightened in her chair and wiped the string of drool from the corner of her mouth. Satisfied that all signs of her snatched sleep had been removed, she called, "Come!"

The door to her sanctum opened.

Osark's balls, it was Jessa. Again. What did the girl want now? She'd already made three visits so far today; the first to tell Alish in minute detail about the state of the Temple pantries. The second to suggest—respectfully of course—that someone should be appointed to have oversight of the candle stores as certain other acolytes were not burning their candles down far enough before replacing them with fresh ones. And the third time to enquire whether Mother Alish's digestion was robust enough for the spiced fish Acolyte Robine intended to prepare for the breaking of next Jansday's fast.

It's a wonder the girl was risking a fourth visit; Mother Alish had made it most clear she did not wish to be disturbed for the rest of the day after the third. And yet here she was . . . again.

Alish sighed inwardly and schooled her features not to show her impatience. "What is it, Jessa?"

The girl approached, her hands clasped together at her waist in a perfect picture of piety. "There are visitors, Mother Alish."

Alish took a deep breath, trying to keep her temper. Was that all? "It is not necessary to inform me about every pilgrim who seeks to pray at our temple, Jessa. Make them welcome, grant them hospitality if they require it, and allow them access to the shrine." Surely the girl had been here long enough to learn the basics? She waved her hand in a gesture of dismissal.

Jessa did not move. "They have requested a private audience."

Alish closed her eyes. "Then go and tell Acolyte Wendolin. She always—"

"With you, esteemed Mother."

No acolyte ever dared to interrupt the Mother. Alish opened her eyes. Jessa looked as shocked as Alish felt.

"Forgive me, Mother, but they insisted. A private audience with you," Jessa whispered. "And I was asked to give you this." She unclasped her hands and extended one of them towards Alish.

For a moment, Alish forgot to breathe.

It had been many years since she'd seen a breeding stone. They had always been secret tokens, used by desperate women to seek the services of women who possessed the knowledge . . .

Slowly she stood, pleased to see that her hand did not shake when she picked the stone carefully from Jessa's palm. "Thank you, Jessa. You may bring the visitors here."

"Yes, Mother." Jessa bowed her head and hurried out, closing the door softly behind herself.

A breeding stone. Alish sank back down, turning the stone over and over. Once they had been common enough, a way of accessing control over one's own womb when the Medix had tightened the laws about reproduction rights. She'd taken control of her own womb, of course; one of the requirements for entering the temple was that she must be a virgin. Her own womb had never been fruitful, but that had been her choice. And now, thank Osark, it had shrivelled to the point where it was unlikely to be of interest to any meddling Medix.

But when the laws had been passed, the breeding stones had been made illegal. Secret places which accepted this most unique currency were raided, the stones confiscated, and women had been forced to bend to the will of the Medix on reproductive issues.

There were still some who recognised the stones . . . who possessed knowledge of reproduction that the Medix either chose to ignore or deemed illegal.

Alish was one of them.

With a swiftness she had almost forgotten she possessed, she moved across the room and pressed one particular point in an otherwise unremarkable and plain wall. There was a click; an outline appeared around a brick. It was then a simple matter to pull the brick free and reach into the space behind it to switch the breeding stone for a thin rod of green metal. Alish hid the latter up her sleeve, then made sure the brick was back in place with no evidence to show it had ever been moved—or that something different now lay in the recess behind it.

She waited impatiently for another knock on the door, the rod weighing down her conscience vastly more than the fabric of her sleeve. She recognised Jessa's knock when it came and and fixed her face to show a neutral expression. "Come."

Jessa opened the door. "Your visitors, Mother Alish." She ushered two women into the sanctum.

A mother and daughter, the mother's face lined with worry, the daughter's full of fear. Perhaps she harboured a guilty secret.

"You may leave us, Jessa. I will ring when my guests are ready to depart."

Alish indicated that her guests should sit and lowered herself back into the heavily carved chair. The mother perched on the edge of her plainer seat and twisted her Joining ring round and round on her finger. The daughter sat beside her, hands clasped tight in her lap, her gaze darting about the room, looking for . . . what? How old was she? Seventeen? Eighteen? No sign of a Joining ring on *her* left hand, though she was certainly old enough to have been wearing one. Much older than normal, in fact, because almost as soon as a girl bled she was considered capable to be Joined and experience the blessing of Fruitfulness. Osark knew, mothers were needed now more than ever, since the Great Decline . . .

"Thank you for accepting my stone, Mother Alish." The mother wasn't wasting any time.

"I will not ask how you knew to associate it with me. It is best that we share as little information as possible, to prevent any repercussions as a result of this audience." Alish's heart stuttered. Was this a trap? A ruse to flush her out, some elaborate hoax to catch her in the act of Divining and root out the last of her kind? She wouldn't put it past the Medix to use some of the old captured stones in that way.

"We need your help, Mother." The mother indicated the daughter. "If her situation continues, there will be accusations laid against her, that she's preventing her own fruitfulness—"

"I'm sure I'm just a late developer. I'll bleed, given time." The girl sounded desperately hopeful.

"You have not yet bled?" The daughter was perfectly developed, had a definite woman's shape. Alish frowned. "But you are what, eighteen? Nineteen?"

"Nineteen next mooncyle," the girl admitted.

Strange.

Alish picked up the Book of Osark from the table beside her chair and held it out to the daughter. "Do you swear, on Osark's Word, that you are not attempting to prevent your own fruitfulness by any means?"

The girl reached out a hand and laid it on the book. "I swear."

"And do you swear, on Osark's Word, that you have never known a man, so cannot be Fruiting at this time?"

"No! I would never . . ." The daughter shook her head and lifted her chin defiantly. "I swear it."

She was in all likelihood telling the truth. The consequences were grave for those who risked bearing Fruit before they were Joined, even though a good harvest seemed to be all that the Medix desired.

A curse on the Medix! A curse on men in general, for laying a woman's entire worth within her womb. Of course the Great Decline needed to be halted, but to force childbearing onto girls barely old enough to leave their dolls behind . . . and to ostracise women who had difficulties in pregnancy or were barren . . . Osark knew that men oft played a role in a lack of offspring; they just never seemed to advertise that fact, preferring to lay blame solely at a female's feet.

"There's something wrong with me, isn't there?"

"Perhaps," Alish admitted, laying the book aside. Her fingertips were tingling, something niggling at her, but what? She dismissed it. "Occasionally the body is broken in some way, but this does not usually become apparent until after the blood comes. And even if there is something wrong, there are treatments . . ." She musn't get the girl's hopes up. There were some things no amount of treatment could resolve. She had no idea what she was dealing with—yet. "First we must discover the truth of the situation. Will you permit an examination?"

The girl flashed a look at her mother, who nodded. "Yes."

"Then come." Alish rose and led the girl to a couch. "Lie there, child."

When the girl was settled, Alish drew the green rod out of her sleeve. "This is old technology, which the Medix choose not to use in its original capacity. It allows me to find your womb and check its health. It will not hurt. See?" She held it loosely in her hand, and it trembled slightly. She passed it down her own body, and it gave a twitch when it passed over her lower belly. Within seconds, a phantom appeared, hanging in the air in front her; a heart shaped vessel with two furred arms reaching towards two small balls. Alish sighed. These organs had done nothing except give her excruciating pain every four weeks for many, many years. Thank Osark they had not bothered her for nigh on a decade. Redundant, but ever-present. "The Medix do not use Divining wands to teach diagnostics now. They use them only to prove the existence of life in a womb—or to demonstrate lack of it."

Which gave them enough evidence to issue fines, oft repeated, when a woman consistently could not bear a child. Gaol was reserved for those unlucky enough to provide proof of life initially and none a little later . . .

Alish gave herself a little shake and smiled at the daughter. "Are you ready? Relax . . ."

She passed the wand over the girl's abdomen, frowned, and repeated the action. No phantom image appeared. Was she out of practice?

"Mother?"

"It's been a while. Give me a moment." She switched the wand to the other hand and wiped it on the edge of her robe. Then she held the rod a little tighter. A third pass . . . still nothing. She passed it over her own body, and the image hung, glittering in the air. One perfectly normal, albeit wizened, womb.

She didn't understand.

"May I . . . ?" Alish approached the mother, passed the rod over *her* abdomen. It worked. Showed a functioning womb, and one ovary stitched to the fallopian tube with scar tissue. This one suffered from Womb-that-travels, where tissues migrated throughout the body, and her womb lining was thick. "You expect to bleed within the next few days?"

The Mother blinked and nodded. "How did you—?"

"I can see it."

The wand was working perfectly well. So why . . . ? Alish turned back to the girl, and suddenly she knew what was niggling at her. There'd been rumours about The Unblooded. Girls who developed normally but never bled, who if the Medix got to know about them, simply disappeared. There were whispers of a cover up, that it was some more serious effect of the Great Decline. Could this be why the Medix had become so fixated on controlling the wombs of women? Because they had used Divining wands and discovered there were girls who did not bleed, who would never bleed, and who could never be fruitful and build up a race so decimated by the conditions that had brought about the Great Decline? How many were affected? And what, in Osark's name, had caused such a phenomenon?

"What can you see, Mother? What is it? What disease keeps me from bleeding?"

"There is no disease," Alish mumbled.

"Oh, thank Osark!"

Alish steeled herself to deliver the truth. "There is no womb, either."

"What?" The girl's eyes widened in shock. She sat bolt upright and looked at her mother.

The mother was staring at Alish. The Mother saw the exact moment when comprehension dawned; her face crumpled, and she fell back into her chair.

"You are hollow, daughter. Hollow!"

Number Nine

Number nine is perfect.

Built as it is, right at the top end of Maggie's Way—a rather poetically named cul-de-sac in the arse-end of town—I have a superb view of all eight of my neighbours.

The bungalow itself is not too shabby. Two bedrooms, one of those open plan living spaces that seem to be all the rage, a kitchen about big enough to swing the proverbial cat, and a bathroom. The thing that sold it to me though, is that everyone's garden is out the front, so what the folk on Maggie's Way get up to is easy enough to keep track of.

I write it all down. In a notebook that I keep by my "watching chair," to record everything I see that's of interest. It's a habit I've cultivated over many years, and I've a stack of notebooks in the bottom of the wardrobe to show for it.

If you're wondering why I do it, well . . . it gives me something to do.

"Unbelievable," my new friend Deidre says. I met her at the corner shop, not long after I moved in. She's taken to coming over once a fortnight, when we share a cuppa, a cake, and a gossip. "You bin doin' it for how long?"

"All my life. Well, since I could write. Fifty-six years now."

It's true, too. I started snooping young, because I was desperate to find out what I wasn't being told by the grown-ups. Once I could write though . . . that was different.

"So, what's gone on this week?" Deidre settles herself into the chair with her mug and a plate.

She's bought cheese scones for a change. I love them when they're warm and soft and the butter goes all melty.

"Well," says I, comfortable in my people-watching spot, where I can see them, but they can't see me. "You know the lass in number five?"

"The one with the itsy bitsy teeny weeny yellow polka dot bikini?"

We had a right laugh over that, we did. Number five's a size twenty if she's anything, and although her bikini is as yellow-dotted as you could want one to be, it certainly isn't very teeny weeny. I still hum the tune under my breath every time I walk past her sunbathing on her lawn though . . ."

"That's the one. Well, I reckon she's having a fling with the milkman."

"Never!"

I nod. "I've seen him pop over there every day this week. I don't reckon she needs that much semi-skimmed, d'you? Especially not at three in the afternoon."

"Not unless she's bathing in the stuff, like Cleopatra!"

We chuckle over that, too.

A proper love shack, number five's got. I'll have to change the tune when I next pass by her garden. See if she notices.

"What else?" Deirdre's all ears, and she's eaten half her scone already.

I make her wait for a bit while I eat mine. "Number six," I say, brushing crumbs off my sweater.

"That's the one who always looks like he's walked out of a fashion ad?"

Always in vogue, number six is. Doesn't matter what the latest fashion is, you can guarantee he'll be wearing it. And I know it's the latest fashion, because I always check on the internet when I see him wearing anything new, to make sure. It must cost an arm and a leg, all that designer stuff, but hey ho. At least he's not spending his money on drugs. I'd know if he was.

"That's the one."

"Well? What about him?"

"Last Wednesday, he hung his washing outside."

"Outside?" Deidre's nose wrinkles as she frowns. "I thought it was number eight that always hung their washing out."

"See? This is why I keep tabs on everyone, Deidre. To spot anything out of the ordinary. And that's why I saw the hoo-ha when Curry's tried to deliver a new washer-drier to number six on Tuesday, wasn't it? He'd gone out that morning, see, wore a rather fetching sea-green suit and a pink satin shirt, so there wasn't anyone in. The driver couldn't leave the machine on the pavement, so he packed it back on the van and drove off."

He hadn't been very happy about it either, after he'd struggled to get it off his van and up the path in the first place. He'd used such language . . . the air was blue.

"I reckon number six must have had problems rearranging the delivery and was getting a bit desperate for undies," I continue, "because

Wednesday he borrowed number eight's rotary to peg out a load of smalls."

"Ooh!" Deidre's eyes widen. "What were they like?"

"Nothing too special." I glance at my notes. "Twenty-five pairs of Calvin Klien boxers, mainly black, with a few pastel shades. But that's not all." I lean forward. "Wednesday last, it rained cats and dogs, didn't it?"

"It did! Did he get his undies in in time?"

"Did he heck as like! He must've been in the shower when he realised, cos he came running out of his front door like Seb Coe after a medal. Deirdre, he was naked in the rain!"

Deidre's crying, she's laughing so hard. I let her wipe her eyes before I move on.

"As if that weren't enough, the joker at number one's added to his collection."

Number one seems to have a thing about garden gnomes. I mean, I've seen *Gnomeo and Juliet*. If number one's gnomes ever came alive and got up to half what those gnomes did in the film, it'd be carnage on the street. It would, I'm telling you. This latest addition brings the count up to forty-three, if the three gnomes playing on a seesaw are all counted separately. It's got more gnomes than grass, that garden.

"Another? What's this one like?"

My turn to frown. "Can't quite work it out. It's got a beard, so I know it's a gnome. But it looks like it's wearing lipstick, a skirt, and platform heels."

Deidre's eyes light up, and she grins. "You never read any Discworld? They have dwarfs there."

"And they dress like that? The dude looks like a lady?"

That sets her off again.

"You daft eejit! No! Lady dwarfs have beards too, in Discworld. And they used to dress like the men, until Cheery Littlebottom came along." She sighs and looks a bit sad. "I miss Sir Terry."

"Wogan?" I'm losing track of this conversation.

"Pratchett."

"Oh." I mull that all over for a bit while I drink my almost cold tea. "Think I prefer the normal gnomes."

"The ones fishing and gardening?" Deirdre's grinning again. "Or the one showing his bum?"

"Yes, well." I bang my mug down. "I don't like any of them, really. I tolerate them."

And occasionally shove the one flashing his backside a little deeper into the shrubbery . . .

"That's everything for now," I say and snap my notebook shut.

"A fair bit going on," says Deidre, nodding. "You know what, Esme? I got a fair few friends who like to keep tabs on things and have a chinwag with me about it, but I can honestly say nothing compares to you."

"I'm one of a kind," I mutter, waving her off later. Deirdre only gets to know what I tell her, you see . . . I'd never share with her the fact that number five and the milkman are actually making saucy videos for a soft porn channel; number one's got a special gnome, hollowed out, where the local drug dealer leaves whatever's been ordered and paid for; and number six has a sugar daddy who pays for all that designer gear. I keep those little nuggets to myself.

Well, not just to myself. People pay good money to keep their sordid little secrets under wraps.

I tend to record *those* things in my *other* notebook . . .

Kinquyakkii

The faces of the three elders were illuminated only by the sparks shooting up from the fire. The villagers, packed tightly into the darkness of the sealskin tent, waited patiently for the men to speak. Eventually, the youngest of the three elders looked up from the flames, his hair still as black as the bird whose name he shared.

"Tonight, there will be war in the heavens," Chulyin announced.

There was a moment of shocked silence before whispers rippled through the gathered people. Ahnah sighed and rolled her eyes.

"No-one must venture outside between sunset and the rise of the dawn star," Isitoq added, his pale eyes still fixed on the dancing flames.

"Yeah, right!"

Miki dug Ahnah in the ribs, warning her to keep quiet.

"Those who do will find themselves in grave peril," Saomik warned as his piercing gaze swept over the assembly and came to a halt when it reached Ahnah.

Discomforted by the old man's stare, Ahnah muttered under her breath. "It's lights in the sky, nothing more."

"Is that what they teach you at school?" Saomik thundered, shocking the room into silence. The last word had sounded almost like a curse as it left his lips. "Do you have no respect at all for the ancient myths?"

"School teaches me plenty," Ahnah snapped. "Kinquyakkii are just lights—"

A collective gasp greeted her announcement and some of the women covered their children's ears.

Ahnah shook her head in disbelief. Did they really fear the truth that much? "I quite fancy seeing them, so I'll be staying up," she added nonchalantly.

Saomik raised his left hand and pointed a gnarled finger at Ahnah.

"Your name means 'wise woman' . . . but you would have been better named 'foolish' if you dare to witness the battle," he said, his voice quivering with rage. "Do not say afterwards that you were not warned."

Ahnah had had enough. With a snort of disgust, she jumped up and pushed her way out of the tent.

The air outside was bitingly cold. Snow sparkled in the light of the twin suns as they sank towards the rim of the world, touching everything with pink and gold while the sky behind them darkened. Soon, it would be night.

"You're not really going to stay up, are you?" Miki caught up with Ahnah and peered, wide-eyed, into his friend's face.

"Course."

Was that admiration or fear in Miki's eyes?

"They're only lights, Miki. Caused by particles from the suns entering the air surrounding our world. They're not what they"—she thumbed over her shoulder to where the villagers were beginning to emerge from the tent—"say. I mean, dragons and angels . . . Come on."

Much later, when the villagers had shut themselves, trembling no doubt, inside their homes, Ahnah was thankful that it wasn't the dead of winter. Her bravado would have been harder to maintain if it had been, even though she'd donned her thickest furs. Sinking her chin deeper into the thick bearskin collar, she wondered if all the aggravation with Saomik had been worth it; it had been an uneventful vigil so far. In spite of herself, Ahnah was disappointed. A million stars had glittered above her head, but no colour had graced the roof of the world. She'd heard of the kinquyakkii of course, but had never seen them. The natural phenomenon rarely came this far south . . .

She shivered. Pulling her coat tighter around her body, she considered whether she could sneak back to her tent without losing face. It couldn't be too long now before the dawn star rose.

Above her, there was a flash of red—gone as quickly as it came.

She stared upwards, wondering if she'd imagined it, but—

"Oh!"

Another flash. A ribbon of green this time, stretching across the sky, ebbing and flowing like coloured water. As the colours intensified, Ahnah's heart quickened.

The red light moved with purpose to her right, shaping itself into a giant creature with slavering jaws . . .

Ahnah pinched herself, hard.

To her left, the green light swirled into a recognisable humanoid form, its outstretched wings dimming the stars behind it.

"No . . . it can't be . . ."

The angel raised an arm, readying the sword of yellow light flickering in its hand as the dragon approached.

Ahnah rubbed her eyes, but it did not erase what she thought she was seeing. She knew the myth, had tried so hard to forget it since her schoolmates had heaped scorn upon it, had preferred the scientific explanation; she remembered it now.

The angels guarded the heavens, prevented the stars from being stolen by the fire dragons. The latter were good at waiting, biding their time in the earthly realm until conditions were favourable to mount an attack. Then they would climb into the sky to retrieve the sparkling treasure they coveted.

The elders always seemed to know when the attack would be . . .

Rooted to the spot as all hell broke loose in the heavens above her, Ahnah could not deny the truth—the reality—of what she was witnessing. She had no idea how long the celestial battle raged, but eventually the angel's sword pierced the dragon's side. The fiery creature twisted in silent agony and melted away, leaving the angel victorious.

The stars were safe—they would shine on! Ahnah cheered and punched her fist into the air.

The cheer died in her throat when the angel turned towards her.

No-one came to find Ahnah until late the next morning. When Soamik slapped the tent flap open, he found her cowering on her bed, shaking as though struck by fever.

"Ahnah?"

Ahnah looked up sharply.

"Soamik?" she almost sobbed. "Where are you?" She reached out desperately. When her questing hand caught hold of the elder, she pulled him close. "Soamik, I can't see you. I can't see anything!"

"What happened?" But Soamik didn't really need to ask. Ahnah's face gave him the answer he had dreaded receiving.

Ahnah's eyeballs were as black as a moonless night, with ribbons of red and green light twisting in their depths.

Puzzle Piece

"Please, won't you cover yourself?"

I'm trying hard not to see, but I can see *everything*. I am used to strangers in my father's house and have seen many things in my time, but this . . .

My father's latest guest leans against the table, testing the effect of her nakedness. "Why?" she asks.

"Because . . . because . . . it is not our custom to expose ourselves." I indicate my own, shapeless gown. Worn by every respectable young woman on my homeworld.

"I have nothing to hide."

Gods, but I wish that were true. My eyes drop to the floor. Calm, Katia. You have dealt with worse. Remember the four-armed Gradat diplomat Father brought home when you were ten? This guest isn't anywhere near as frightening as that. She's humanoid for a start. Just like you.

She's nothing like you! my brain screams. *If you had her courage, her self-assurance, her beauty . . . your life would be so different.*

When I find the courage to lift my gaze, she's watching me with eyes as green as the jewels resting on her forehead. Is she measuring me? Against what standard? A spark of anger flares briefly in my chest before it dies. Will she find me lacking? Like so many others?

Her eyes look deep into me, probing, seeking . . . Blink, Katia! Break the spell! Focus instead on the lines drawn across her golden skin, on the coloured fragments dotted randomly between them. My fingers twitch. Keen, it seems, to trace those myriad patterns.

"Are they . . . painted?"

She shakes her head, which sets the black-green feathers at her throat and in her hair fluttering.

"Inked, then?" A ripple of imagined pain runs through me at the thought of hours spent suffering at the hands of the tattooist.

Another shake. I could swear those feathers are alive.

She runs a finger along her flank. "We are created this way. At birth, our skins are empty, like yours."

Is that a statement of fact, or condemnation? I'm not sure.

"They develop over time, writing our destinies in their patterns," she continues. "The reading of the destinies is a privilege granted to very few of my people."

"Can you? Read them, I mean?"

This time she nods and almost smiles. "I can."

I feel myself frowning and make a conscious effort to smooth out the lines. It's a habit borne from years of Father snapping "Katia! You look like an old woman. Smile!" But I am puzzled. And suddenly, inexplicably, afraid. "Why has my father invited you here? We don't have lines for you to read."

Again that look, measuring me. "Because I can read futures without lines."

"You're going to read my father's future?" The tears that never seem to be far away nowadays stick in my throat. Does he really need an off-worlder to tell us what we already know? That he is going to die—soon—of the creeping weakness? How many more times will he need to hear it before he accepts it?

"No," this guest with the patterned skin whispers. "Katia, I have come to read yours."

Washing Day

The thick burlap wrap in which the Washing Cloths had arrived fell open. Each of the cloths were wrapped separately in more burlap, as was the custom, but Tessi's heart stuttered when she lifted the first cloth free.

Underneath it was something wrapped in a protective layer of black lambswool.

Time stretched long and thin as Tessi carefully laid the cloth on the table and stared at the alien object. She'd thought her little flock was safe. Had only ever received the lambswool package once, in her first year, *before* she'd had a chance to build relationships in the village.

"Daughter? Are you there?"

Tessi snatched up the object and shoved it into the folds of her skirt where it weighed down her pocket far less than it weighed on her mind. "Come in, Ailsa."

The blanket at the door was swept aside.

"Have they come?" Ailsa's eyes shone with excitement.

Tessi forced herself to smile. How well she remembered birthing Ailsa in the depths of winter, pulling her reluctantly from the warmth of her mother's womb, the squalling newborn yelling and raging as only a newborn can against being dragged into the cold. Would Ailsa yell and rage again, fifteen years later, if . . . ?

She gave herself a shake. It might not be Ailsa. There were two cloths this time.

"Just arrived." Tessi pointed and Ailsa skipped across to the table to look.

"Which one's mine?"

Tessi shrugged. "It doesn't matter. They're both the same," she lied.

Ailsa flung her arms around Tessi and squeezed her tight. "I'm so excited, Daughter! After my Washing, I shall be Linked!"

Tessi nodded. "I know." Gently she pulled away from Ailsa's embrace. "Kody is a good man, Ailsa. You will be much blessed, I'm certain."

How could she even speak these words without them turning to ash and dust in her mouth? She marvelled at her own duplicitousness even as nausea churned her gut like butter. She pressed it down with a hand to her stomach. She had trained for this eventuality, knew she must not give any sign. The Great Amma was depending on her.

Ailsa cocked her head. "Will I still look pretty d'you think, in a plain shift?"

Tessi laughed. Couldn't help it. How like Ailsa, to forget that when she did wear the shift, her whole world might be changed in an instant. "Child, you'd look good in a sack. The Great Amma gave you red hair and green eyes for a reason."

"She did, didn't she?" Ailsa twirled on the spot and then staggered to a stop. "I must tell Clara!"

She was off then, like a startled hare. Tessi stood at the door, watching the child's long legs flashing under her skirt as she ran to tell her best friend the news. Then she turned slowly back inside. Time to thread her needle.

It took almost no time at all to sew the shifts—they were shapeless things after all, with straight seams along their sides and across the shoulders. Yet hours passed before Tessi completed the task, thanks to the steps necessary to prevent cross-contamination.

Working on only one piece of fabric at a time. Scrubbing the table with natrace. Burning the burlap sacks she spread across her lap to protect her skirts. Melting down the silver needles after every session of sewing, and storing the minute—purified—beads, ready to be resurrected as new needles. Sealing the completed garments in paper wrappings and writing the recipient's name on them.

The worst part was soaking her hands in the dilute natrace every time she finished handling the fabric. Thank Amma there were only two shifts to make, because well before the second was finished, Tessi had already scratched at her itching skin until she bled. What must it be like for other Daughters, who received the lambswool-wrapped package and had to make many more shifts for *their* Washing Days?

She tried not to think about which of the two garments she'd sewn was the one.

"Thank you, Daughter," Clara whispered, taking the parcel from Tessi as though it was something immensely fragile.

"May Great Amma be with you tomorrow." Tessi turned away.

"Daughter!"

Tessi fought the urge to run, to distance herself from this moment. She'd faced it before of course—the girls all reacted in different ways on receiving their shifts and many of them were understandably nervous. But she'd never had to offer reassurance, knowing what she knew this time. Slowly she turned back. "Yes, Clara?"

Clara's eyes were bright with tears. "Do you think . . . ?" She swallowed. "Do you think I'll wash clean, Daughter?"

"Only the Great Amma knows, child."

The words were glib and well practised, and they hid the truth.

Ailsa received her own parcel with rather more delight, hugging it to her chest and dancing around the yard with her hair flying out behind her like a banner.

"I shall be washed clean and then Linked," Ailsa told Tessi when she finally stopped twirling. "Clara's going to be my Maid at the Linking, because she doesn't even have a beau yet. We shall both have arta flowers woven into our hair, and we'll wear soft silk slippers for the dancing, and I shall be Kody's breath and he will be mine!"

Tessi couldn't bear it. "May Great Amma be with you tomorrow," she muttered, and walked away as quickly as she could without running.

At dawn on Washing Day, Daughter Tessi wrapped herself in a thick wool cloak to ward off the early morning chill. Then she reached into the little nook behind the stove, where she'd hidden the lambswool and its contents. She threw the wool into the stove, where it smouldered for a moment on the still-warm ashes before bursting into flame and shrivelling to nothing. The glass ampoule it had been protecting went into Tessi's pocket.

The walk to the sacred pool was not a long one, but with every step taken, the weight of responsibility fell heavier on Tessi's shoulders. Finally she reached the pool and knelt beside it. It was the work of a moment to snap the ampoule open and pour the perfectly clear liquid it contained into the opaque green water.

"Great Amma, choose wisely the next of your Daughters."

Now all she could do was wait.

It was late afternoon when the Collecting Daughters arrived, the green lines tattooed on both their faces a visible reminder of their special position. They came to every Washing Day of course, but apart from Tessi's first year as this flock's Daughter, they had always gone away empty-handed.

Until now.

This time, their hands would be full.

Washing Days were always a community affair. Everyone from the village came to watch, and afterwards, there would be a feast. A celebration, because Great Amma had blessed the girls and granted them womanhood.

Tessi had no idea how she would manage to eat afterwards, knowing that only one family would be celebrating.

As sunset approached, Daughter Tessi, now wearing her ceremonial cape—the one embroidered with the symbols of Great Amma and womanhood—walked over the bridge, the excited chatter of the assembled villagers audible even from this distance. The two girls walked on either side of her.

Ailsa sighed. "Our bridge is so ordinary."

And it was; just rough-hewn stones, carved by a heavy hand and shaped into a simple arch over the stream which fed the pool.

"It does not need to be ornate," Tessi told her sharply. "It's symbolic."

Ailsa tossed her hair over her shoulder. "Because we're crossing into womanhood. I know. But it would've been nice to have a more beautiful one to walk over. What do you think, Clara?"

The day's warmth lingered, but Clara seemed unaware of it; she was shivering when Tessi glanced down at her.

The girl was still nervous, then.

The noise level rose and eager faces turned as Daughter Tessi and her charges walked the last section of path and came to a halt at the pool's side.

Tessi lifted her hand and silence fell.

"Once a girl reaches fifteen years, she is washed," she said. "The sacred pools are blessed by Great Amma through her Daughters, so that during the Washing, the water will decide whether the girl is clean and worthy to enter and enjoy the joy of womanhood. If the water decides otherwise, Great Amma gains a new Daughter." She paused, checking that the Collecting Daughters had taken up their positions beside the pool steps. "Let the Washing begin. Clara. You will wash first."

Clara appeared frozen, fear etched deep on her face.

And then Tessi saw it; the bulge in the girl's belly that was so at odds with the rest of her skinny frame, and barely hidden by the loose ceremonial shift. Quick as a flash, she scanned the faces in the crowd. Who—?

There! Sidnay Horith, paler than he'd ever been, guilt writ large across his features. So that was the way of it. There'd have to be a Linking—and fast. But only if . . .

Suddenly, Ailsa grabbed Clara's hand. "We've done everything together up to now. Let's wash together, too." She tugged Clara towards the pool, past the Collecting Daughters, down the steps, and into the murky water.

Tessi's breath caught in her throat as both the red head and the brown disappeared under the green water once, twice, three times. Great Amma, which one would it be? She couldn't bear to watch. She shut her eyes as acid fear burned her stomach. Great Amma, let it only be one . . . Surely you aren't cruel enough to demand *two* new Daughters from my small flock?

It was the only way to supply Great Amma with Daughters of course; it removed choice. Why would a girl—a woman—voluntarily give up being Linked, and the chance to bear children? How could a Daughter decide on who to lose from her flock if it was demanded of her? It would be too tempting to protect those she loved and respected; to let go of and lose those she did not favour. No. It was better this way, even if it meant that at least one of the girls she'd watched growing up for the last fifteen years would emerge from the pool bearing a sign so life changing . . .

She forced her eyes open.

The required number of submersions had been completed. All part of the ceremony, but in reality designed to ensure the various chemicals were thoroughly agitated.

Ailsa was first to climb out of the water. She stood, dripping, on the top step.

A wail rose from the crowd, was quickly stifled.

"No," Ailsa whispered, staring at her poisonous green shift. "No!"

The Collecting Daughters grabbed hold of her before she could run.

All eyes turned towards Clara; her disbelief was obvious as she emerged from the green water, plucking at her own still-white garment.

"No!" Ailsa screamed. "She should have the green! Not me! I'm to be Linked! Clara has no man!"

Oh, but she did, she did. And if Clara *had* been the one to emerge wearing the green, she'd have gone from this village, supposedly to become a Daughter of Amma . . . but Great Amma would never have accepted her. Not now. Not after Sidnay…

"Clara, you are now a woman and blessed by Great Amma." Tessi had to shout so that she could be heard over Ailsa's screams. "Go, celebrate your future!"

Then she forced herself to look upon the girl whose dreams she had helped to shatter. Would she remember the words required of her at this moment? She hadn't needed to speak them for nigh on twenty years . . .

"Ailsa, Great Amma has chosen you to be one of her Daughters. Go from this place and set aside your life for her service. May Great Amma protect you."

Although she failed to protect me when my own Washing Day shift turned the same colour, she added silently, watching as the Collecting Daughters dragged Ailsa—still screaming for her mother, for Kody, for a chance to get into the pool and wash again—away.

Great Amma, in whose name fifteen-year-old girls were taken from their homes to the temple, to have their hopes of love and husbands and children beaten out of them.

Great Amma, whose initiated Daughters were taught how to sew only one shift at a time because of the chemicals applied to certain Washing Cloths.

Great Amma, who caused all her Daughters, when assigned to their flocks, to live in fear of a lambswool-wrapped ampoule.

Great Amma, in whose name women called Daughters acted as unwilling midwives, overseeing the birth of future Daughters.

Great Amma.

A fantasy of maternal care.

Peas in a Pod

I kneel beside the cage. Reaching between the bars, I stroke the hair of the slumbering form within. She stirs, but does not wake.

"You're like two peas in a pod. Both beautiful," Father says. "Are you sure you wouldn't rather keep her?"

"Why?" I withdraw my hand and rise slowly to my feet. "I have no need of her now, do I?"

Father shrugs. "You could present her as a novelty occasionally." He catches hold of my left hand. Turns it over and smooths a thumb across the mark on the inside of my wrist . . . checking.

I manage not to snatch my hand away and shake my head. "It would cause confusion. What if those you rejected were to discover the deception you orchestrated?"

He sighs. "Very well. If you are sure, I shall make the necessary arrangements."

He plants a dry kiss on my forehead, which I tolerate, reminding myself it is one of only a few more I must endure from Him. Soon, there will be passionate kisses—from Andreth . . .

Within the cage, the creature's eyes have opened, their gaze strangely unfocused. I see myself reflected in them and smile. Her face may be my face, but there the similarities end. We have very different pasts behind us, and very different futures ahead.

She was born naturally, you see. Lived for twenty privileged years before the necessity of the marriage mart and Father's genius granted me life. I shudder at the memory of twenty years of growth and development, condensed into a few short, laboratory-based months. And then, in order for the duplicate to be utterly convincing, Father added emotion, intelligence, and independent thought to His manufactured flesh-and-bone body . . .

He kept only one thing different, so He might tell us apart.

When He deemed me to be ready, He explained that my sole purpose was to act the part of His true-born daughter in a quest to find potential mates without compromising either her virtue or her value.

But He never seemed to consider that, thanks to Him, His creation might subsequently discover love. And desire. And the desperate longing to live.

Everything Father created me to be, I have used against Him. Which is why His own daughter lies drugged within the cage, with her distinctive birthmark camouflaged . . . destined for destruction.

And why I, her near-perfect clone with an unusual tattoo on my wrist, am standing outside . . . where I will remain.

Potato Soup

Agneta's bags fell to the floor with a thump.

"Is this it?" She stared in disbelief at the bare walls, the curtainless window, and stained floor of the single room and her bottom lip trembled. "I want to go home."

"We can't." Gregor's tone was flat. "You know we can't. Pa wanted us safe. Better to be living here than suffering back there, don't you think?"

"Don't!" A hot prickle stung Agneta's eyes, and she tried to blink it away, prevent the tears from falling. Throughout the journey she'd tried not to think of the friends and neighbours who hadn't listened, who'd decided to trust The Elite and were most likely dead or slaves by now. Pa's decision might have saved her life, but Agneta hadn't expected this. She wiped away a leaked tear and sighed. "You're right, Greg. Of course, you are. But there's nothing here. Nothing." She shivered. "And it's cold."

"We'll be home before you know it," Pa said, as he struggled into the room with the trunk. He set it down with a groan.

Hope flared in Agneta's chest. "You mean we can go back?"

Pa shook his head. "Not while The Elite rule. I meant that we can make here our home."

Agneta's face must've shown her disappointment and disbelief, because Pa beckoned her to him and put an arm around her shoulders. "Look around you, Aggi. What do you see?"

"Nothing, Pa. There's nothing here. Except me, you, and Greg."

"Are you sure? Look again. Tell me, what do you see?"

"Bare walls, curtainless window, stained floor, stove," she began. Then paused. Stove? Yes. A small pot-bellied stove she hadn't noticed before. Was there anything else? "A table in that corner, two stools under it . . . box beds . . ."

"See?" Pa gave her a little shake. "All of the basics in one room. Right now, it's empty, but we are going to make it ours. Shall we get started?"

By suppertime the room had been transformed.

The stove was lit, its orange belly radiating warmth to both the inhabitants of the room and a pot which Agneta had left bubbling gently on the hotplate.

"Nothing like the smell of potato soup to make you feel right at home," Pa said, breathing in a great lungful.

Perhaps. It wasn't just the soup and the stove, though. Slowly, Agneta's gaze took in the changes.

Now, there was a curtain—of a sort—at the window. No-one else would know it was really her second-best underskirt, tacked above the lintel and hooked out of the way until darkness fell.

On the freshly scrubbed table, a simple lantern cast a warm glow in the previously dark corner, a sturdy log pulled up beside it to serve as a third stool for Gregor. Three sturdy earthenware bowls, three plain spoons, and three wooden cups set out in readiness, hinted at the supper to come.

A hint of lavender hung in the air, released from the linen and blankets now laid upon the newly made beds. Atop them lay the quilts—joining ceremony presents from Grandmare for Ma and Pa from so long ago. On the bed that was to be Agneta's lay her favourite quilt; a ring of stars in shades of gold and cream on a background of midnight blue. Thank goodness Pa had thought to bring them all. Not just for their warmth, but because each quilt was a miniature family history; a piecing together of dresses worn and torn and grown out of, of too-short trouser legs, and shirts too worn to be mended, mixed with precious offcuts of outfits made by Grandmare in the days when she was a seamstress to the wealthy.

The only new piece of furniture was the shelf. And on the simple plank lying across two upright logs were the family's most precious possessions.

Pa had left many other things behind in favour of these and for a moment, Agneta allowed herself to remember some of them . . . The silver teapot and matching milk jug that was always used for birthday teas. The ornate candlesticks at either end of the mantel that had been handed down by Pa's family for generations. The pictoframes of family faces long dead. The leather-bound books in the library, including the one filled with fairy tales that she'd loved so much. Her favourite peacock blue beaded dress with the matching kitten-heeled slippers . . .

Remembering would not make them suddenly appear. None of those things had been practical and Pa had packed only the essentials when they left. So, the only things sitting on the shelf were two books, a single pictogram, and Pa's pipe and tobaccy tin. Agneta ran her finger slowly down the spine of *The Regulo*, the code by which they both lived and were persecuted. Next to it stood *The History of the Armenta*, a thick tome telling the story of her people. The pictogram was Ma, taken in happier times, sitting in a meadow with her skirt pooled around her and her hair hanging loose about her shoulders. She hadn't lived to see the Elite's persecution of the Armenta, or make this journey. Agneta couldn't decide whether that was a good or bad thing.

"It's better, isn't it?" Pa's voice broke into her thoughts. He was watching her.

She shrugged. "I suppose. Still not home, though."

"Really?" Pa swept out his arm, encompassing the room and its contents. "We have *The Regulo* and no-one in this place to tell us we cannot follow it. We have plenty to remind us of the past and the place we came from." His voice softened. "We have food and warmth and each other, and the here and now. What more do you want, Aggi?"

"I want our house," she whispered, her eyes prickling again. "I want our village, my friends, everything we had . . . I want to go home." A solitary tear tracked down her cheek.

"A house does not make a home, Aggi," Pa told her gently. "We become attached to one place, it's true, but you can make anywhere your home if you take the most important bits with you when you travel." He looked round, smiling, though his eyes were full of pain. "This will be home. One day."

Agneta wiped her cheek dry with the back of her hand and looked round the room again. It didn't feel like home, not really, not yet. But she understood. And maybe, one day . . .

One day.

She smiled weakly. Best get on with it, then. "Potato soup, anyone?"

The Pink Feather Boa Incident

"Excuse me? I think you dropped something?"

Paul turned towards the man who'd stopped him and half-smiled, half-frowned at the pink feather being held out to him. "Nope, not me."

"Are you sure, Paul? It *is* Paul, isn't it?"

The man was persistent, the voice vaguely familiar, but he couldn't place it. "Do I know you?"

It was Amelie who recognised him. Oh, there was now a paunch, and thinning hair, but the face was etched onto her memory, even if Paul didn't remember . . .

"We were students together." The man stepped closer, pocketing the feather. "Business Studies and Finance, about . . . twenty-five years ago?"

Twenty-seven, Amelie whispered, but Paul didn't listen. He didn't listen to her very much at all, these days.

"Oh, right." Paul frowned. "I'm sorry, I don't remember you."

The stranger's face darkened momentarily. "Richard. Richard Fraser."

"Richard. How are you doing?" He had no idea who this man was, whether he'd studied with him or not, but he shook hands with him anyway.

Amelie winced at the contact.

"Not as well as you, it seems." Richard nodded towards the glass and steel building in whose shadow they stood. Three-foot-high letters above the entrance spelled out Hemming Finance.

Paul shrugged. "I worked hard, got lucky a few times."

"Yeah, looks like it."

Was there a hint of jealousy wrapped around those words? If so, Paul chose to ignore it.

"Always said you'd go far. Not like me. Saw the article in *Hello*, by the way. What was it they voted you? Finance wizard and most eligible bachelor of the decade, wasn't it? I'm pleased for you."

Amelie noticed that Richard's smile didn't seem to reach his eyes and she shuddered.

Paul glanced at his Rolex, keen to get on, get away from this man who appeared to know an awful lot about him but was still a stranger. "Thanks. Look, sorry to cut this short, but I have a ten o'clock meeting. Nice to see you again, Richard. All the best." He turned away, mind already on the job, and walked towards his workplace.

"Yeah, you too. Perhaps we can meet up some time? Have a proper catch up?" Richard called after him. "Bring Amelie and—"

The door swung shut behind Paul, cutting off the rest.

Two days later, the first envelope arrived.

"Excuse me. Mr Hemming?"

Paul glanced up from the analysis of Barty Leminster's holdings. "Yes?"

Cecile stepped quickly towards the desk. "This just arrived. Marked confidential."

He gestured towards the in-tray. "Why do they bother? Leave it, I'll check it in a bit."

Ten minutes after Cecile left, he signed off Barty's documents—how much gold could one man need?—and reached for the letter. It amused him that some of his clients still insisted on sending their paperwork to him personally, as though unaware that their business deals were actually handled by his portfolio managers. But Paul had gotten into the habit of opening all the correspondence marked "confidential" anyway, because a client whose finances were handled personally, albeit for mere seconds, by Mr Hemming himself, seemed to keep coming back. So, he opened the envelope and grinned. How much would its contents add to his turnover this time?

At first, he thought it was a joke, that the envelope was empty, but then he caught sight of the feather. He pulled the bright pink thing out and an old dread settled, heavy, in his stomach.

Then he dropped both feather and envelope into the bin.

Three days later, another envelope arrived, identical to the first. Marked confidential. This time, the pink feather was stuck to a small card, on which was written a short message and a phone number.

Amelie owes me, it said.

Paul's gut churned, but for the first time in a long while, he allowed himself to remember . . .

And then he waited.

For a whole week, his heart raced every time Cecile dropped any post into his in-tray, but there were no more envelopes marked confidential. He began to relax, to think the danger had passed, when the third one arrived.

Inside was a sheet of folded paper and the inevitable pink feather.

Paul peeled the paper open. His chest tightened, he couldn't breathe—but he couldn't stop looking.

Someone had gone to great lengths to mock up the front page of *The Sun*. FINANCE FRAUD screamed the headline, and Amelie's face filled the space underneath.

The photographer had caught her mid-laugh, head thrown back in gleeful abandon, champagne glass in hand; "It's not a party without champagne, darling!" It had always sounded like a battle cry to Paul . . .

His breathing easier now, he stroked Amelie's cheek on the page. How unencumbered she'd been, like a bird set free from its cage, the life and soul of every party. No wonder he'd been drawn to her. She'd been everything he wanted to be, instead of the studious young man, trapped and wrapped in numbers and equations, that he'd become. Still was, if he was honest.

He remembered perfectly the night the picture had been taken, because Amelie was wearing the bloody pink feather boa, the one she'd picked up for pennies in the flea market that very morning. It had tickled his nose and shed feathers everywhere, but she'd loved it. She'd worn it that evening while she drank gallons of champagne and then wrapped it round the neck of—

"Richard Fraser," Paul murmured. "Shit!"

The name hit him with the force of a well-placed punch, winding him afresh as he remembered the balding stranger holding out a pink feather. He crumpled the paper and threw it at the wall, sudden anger burning hot in his chest. *That* Richard? Why the hell hadn't Amelie tipped him off? Or had she tried, and—like normal—he'd ignored her, like he so often did these days? He'd been so careful to keep her out of his new world, allowing her only the rarest of forays back into the bright lights of London nightlife that she used to love so much.

Paul ran a hand over his face, trying to think.

Twenty-seven years ago, Richard Fraser had scared them. He'd started hanging round Paul in the last year of uni in a vain attempt to pick up enough information to avoid a Third degree from the student most likely to gain a First. He'd met Amelie purely by chance when she'd decided to celebrate graduation early; for a while Paul had thought everything would be alright, watching from a distance as Amelie flirted with Richard but kept him at arm's length.

But Richard had been persistent. The . . . what to call it? Affair? Infatuation? Paul wasn't sure. Whatever formed the root of the connection that Amelie and Richard had had, it continued to grow long after the proper graduation ceremony, right up to the night of what Paul referred to as The Pink Feather Boa Incident. He couldn't remember all the details—perhaps he'd deliberately blocked them from his memory—but he knew that Richard had got too close that night and threatened to tear Amelie's world apart. Sensible Paul had come to the rescue, forced her to leave the club, the unpaid-for champagne—and Richard Fraser—behind.

The recent accidental meeting, the feathers in the envelopes; everything stemmed from that night. Paul was certain of it. He was certain of something else, too. Having successfully avoided Amelie for the longest period of time to date, he was going to have to talk to her about Richard.

And soon.

"We can't let him ruin everything I've worked for and built because of you." Paul knew that would hurt Amelie, but he didn't feel like holding back. She was fully aware that she embarrassed him, always had been. She'd done her best to live with the restrictions he placed on her, and he was grateful for that. Things had been going well recently, since he hadn't seen so much of her.

But now, Richard threatened everything. He was too large a pebble to be chucked into what had been a still pond; the ripples of potential consequence were simply too big to ignore.

"We have to do something," Paul said.

Amelie spoke for the first time. "Well, I started this. I suppose I ought to finish it."

Finish it? Paul frowned. "What?"

"We'll have to get rid of him."

The certainty in her voice sent a trickle of fear down Paul's spine. "What do you mean?" And yet deep down he knew full well, had suspected what Amelie the confident, Amelie the strong, Amelie the uninhibited, would suggest. "Not . . . ? I can't! What if—?"

Amelie sighed. "I know you can't. Why don't you stick to your numbers, and leave dealing with Richard to me? Hmm?"

At that moment, he both loved and hated her in equal measure. Loved her for being capable of doing what he was too weak to do himself. Hated her for the same reason. But could he let go of the situation, allow her to take control? The thought of what he could lose if Richard's mock newspaper headlines ever hit the real tabloids decided him. Reluctant, but secretly relieved, Paul nodded.

"I'd better get on, then." Amelie grinned and stretched in that cat-like way she had, sending a shiver of anticipation down Paul's spine. "You said there was a phone number?"

The razor slid easily over Amelie's skin and she followed it with her hand, checking for stray hairs. It would be no good snagging her stockings as soon as she put them on. Satisfied with a job well done, she rose from the water—

"Like Venus from the waves," she murmured.

—and patted herself dry as the bubbles and stubble drained away.

She applied the makeup carefully, camouflaging the tell-tale signs that she wasn't twenty-one anymore. A slick of lipstick to finish and—

"Perfect." She blew a kiss at her reflection and laughed. How long had it been since she'd done this? She was going to savour every second of it.

Richard was waiting at the bar when Amelie arrived. She saw his eyes widen and heard his low whistle as she sashayed towards him, the simple but oh-so-elegant silk wrap dress clinging to her body and cool against her skin, her slingback heels the perfect height to emphasise her shapely calves. She'd been careful not to overdo things, of course. To show him that she wasn't the same flighty creature she'd been then, but someone he could still desire.

"Hello, Richard."

"Amelie. I didn't think you'd come."

He offered champagne and she sipped it slowly, keeping him waiting, aware of the power she still held over him. Maybe that's why she hadn't given him up all those years ago. Well, not until Paul had forced her to. She'd always loved feeling powerful. With a jolt, she realised that she and Paul were more alike than either of them had ever realised . . .

"I was in two minds for a while," she said eventually. "But Paul agreed it was for the best. He sent you this." She pulled the brown envelope from her clutch bag, careful not to pull out the other thing with it, and held it out. Richard looked puzzled. "It's payback for all the champagne I drank that night. I think you'll find he's been most generous. Debt paid."

She watched as Richard checked the contents before slipping the envelope into his pocket.

"I thought Paul"—Richard laid a subtle emphasis on the name—"would have given more to keep your . . . association with him under wraps." His eyes ran over her body, while his tongue ran over his lips.

Amelie smiled. She'd known that money wouldn't be enough to ensure there were no further repercussions. Richard's undisguised and years-old unfulfilled lust would play right into her hands. She dropped a hand onto his thigh. "I seem to remember I left you before things could get . . . interesting," she purred. "Shall we allow ourselves an interesting evening at last, Richard?"

So she wined and dined him, noting with pleasure the open stares of jealous women and the sly looks of envious men. Twenty-seven years and she'd not lost her touch. She sparkled as much as the champagne she pretended to drink, gauging the moment when Richard could be persuaded to leave for the hotel.

It was a discrete establishment, used on the few occasions over the years that she'd braved the outside world and left Paul behind in the apartment. Tonight, the reception staff merely nodded politely, completely ignoring the fact that Amelie was all but carrying Richard across the lobby to the lift.

They got out on the second floor.

"Here we are . . ." Amelie propped Richard against the wall while she opened the door with a good old-fashioned key.

He stumbled over the threshold, then spun round, reaching for her. He pulled her close. "Gonna give you what I wanted to," he slurred, "before you ran out on me."

His kiss bruised Amelie's mouth. "Bed," she whispered, knocking the door shut behind them. Richard held her tight as she pushed him further into the room.

She broke free of him, kicked off her shoes, and threw her bag into a chair. Next to go was the dress, slipping over her shoulders and sliding to the floor. Richard groaned and reached for her again but she dodged out of reach.

"Not yet, eager beaver." Amelie picked up the discarded bag.

The pink feather might have been made of lead for the effect it had on Richard; at its first touch, he fell back onto the bed and opened his arms to her.

"D'you remember the boa, Richard?" Amelie whispered as she straddled him, running the tip of the feather along the blurred contours of his face.

"You should have worn it tonight." Richard tightened his hold on her waist and ground his solid dick into her crotch. His eyes closed and he let out a long, low moan.

That's when Amelie reached for the pillow.

When it was over, when she was absolutely sure the threat had passed, Amelie rolled off the bed, staggered into the bathroom, and was violently sick.

At last, she wiped her mouth, lifted her head, and breathed deeply as the enormity of what she'd done sank in. Paul had thought her strong, but he'd been wrong. Richard had almost bested her.

She stared at herself in the mirror, its unforgiving strip light revealing smears in the carefully applied makeup, scratches on her arms, a torn bra strap, and a faint shadow along her jawline. She'd come so close to losing . . .

Then again, maybe she'd already lost. After tonight, she'd have to disappear for good. For Paul's sake.

Amelie stared into the mirror. "You're safe," she murmured, pulling off the wig.

A tear-streaked, scratched, and bruised Paul stared back.

"Thank you," he said, his relief obvious as Amelie ripped a couple of pieces of toilet paper off the roll and began to wipe away every trace of her existence.

The Memory of Amelia Maybelove

Amelia Maybelove stood as tall as she could, which wasn't easy.

She'd been blessed with many things, had Amelia—a good eye, a quick hand, a keen nose, an eidetic memory—but height was not one of them. Even so, she would not allow the scorching gaze of Master Bentley to cause her to shrink further.

The Hall of Judgement held the sort of silence that can only ever be made by over two hundred girls holding their breath. Amelia could feel their eyes on her back, watching, waiting. How many of them had done worse than she had, to earn a place in the Sam Bentley Correctional School for Girls? And how many had done less . . . ?

"So."

The single word dropped into that silence, spreading ripples of fear through its audience. Even Amelia felt a shiver, in spite of her promise to herself, that she would not give any of the Masters the satisfaction of seeing how scared witless she was.

"Amelia Maybelove, you stand before us—" Master Bentley indicated the men sitting either side of him behind the wide oak table.

To his right, Master Crastor: fat rolls pouring over his high collar, stomach straining jacket buttons to bursting point, dabbing with a giant handkerchief the sweat beading his forehead.

To his left, Master Hodkins: skeletal, grey-skinned, peering at her over the top of his seeing-eyes. A veritable husk of a man.

Amelia's eyes slid back to Master Bentley. If you'd met him in any other place, you'd think him a handsome man. Good jaw, strong cheekbones, no grey in his hair. Plus an edge of flint in his eyes and a hint of cruelty at the corner of his mouth . . . He was still talking.

"—your actions. You have come here direct from the perfumery, have you not?"

Amelia cleared her throat. "Yes," she said, quickly adding "master" when he frowned.

"Would you care to explain to the assembled company what you did that has brought you here?"

The Master already knew—they all did—but actually saying it, owning up to it, made Amelia squirm.

"I made a perfume," she muttered, looking at her feet.

"Louder."

"I made a perfume." There. It didn't sound so bad, now she'd said it.

"But it was not a... pleasant... perfume, was it, Amelia Maybelove?"

"It was."

"Speak up!"

She snapped her head up. "It was! To begin with, anyway. Hints of honeysuckle and vanilla and honey, sweet and heady. Then..." She paused.

"Then?"

How could she possibly explain? That floral and spicy notes were not enough for her? That she had a desire to extract the essence of aroma from everything? Her experimentation with essential oils of garlic... fish guts... soilheaps... It had been a challenge; no-one had ever created a polyodorous perfume. Single, pure scents, yes. Blended scents, yes. But one that changed over time, that smelled steadily worse instead of better... no.

Until she'd made hers.

"Amelia Maybelove! Answer! And then what?"

"Um..." She wrinkled her nose as she remembered the sequence, almost as though she were smelling it again. "Boiled cabbage."

"Silence!" Master Bentley roared as titters broke out through the hall.

That sound gave Amelia the courage to continue. "After that, rotten egg, like the worst farts imaginable. And then..." She warmed to the telling, encouraged by the girls' open laughter. At least they appreciated her skill. She raised her voice. "My pièce de résistance. Spoiled meat. It's all in the chemistry."

Masters Bentley, Crastor, and Hodkins did their utmost to restore order. But their demands for silence fell on deaf ears, and it was only when the inmates were threatened with academy-wide repercussions that the room eventually fell quiet.

Two spots of livid colour burned in Master Bentley's cheeks. "Tell me," he said to Amelia, his voice deceptively quiet, "was it worth it?"

She had nothing to lose now. "Oh yes! You should have seen them, the ladies, grabbing the free samples. And how they came running back, gagging and heaving! They didn't appreciate the workmanship, the skill—"

"The perfumier you were apprenticed to has been ruined," Master Crastor interrupted. "The compensation . . ." He broke into a fresh sweat.

"Such disruptive behaviour will not be tolerated," Master Hodkins added, his voice as dry and cracked as his skin.

"We will judge." The three Masters leaned close to each other and spoke in whispers.

Time slowed as Amelia waited. She was acutely aware of the girls at her back. She would most likely be joining them until she'd worked off her debt to the perfumier.

It didn't take the Masters long to decide. When they leaned back in their seats, it was Master Bentley who spoke.

"We have reached our decision. Amelia Maybelove, you will be cleansed by thoughtfish."

A collective gasp sucked Amelia backwards two steps. All her bravado disappeared.

"No, please!" She shook her head, trembling in every limb. "Not a thoughtfish . . ."

"You will remain incarcerated in the Sam Bentley Correctional Facility for Girls," the Master continued, as though she had not spoken, "until we are certain that all knowledge relating to the preparation of perfume, including any personally derived recipes, has been removed."

Amelia's skin prickled. "But what'll I do then? Perfume's the only thing I know. I'll have no way of making a living—"

"You should have thought of that before." The Master made a movement with his hand.

Strong hands gripped Amelia's arms and legs, lifting, carrying, until she lay pinned to the very table at which the Masters sat.

"No! I'm sorry! Please—I'll not do it again, I promise!"

Three or four young women held her fast as another approached, carrying a jar filled with writhing silver-green worms.

Amelia thrashed and fought right up until the moment the tongs, with a single wriggling thoughtfish held captive in them, touched her nostril; that's when she screamed and fell still.

The Masters watched Amelia Maybelove closely, until her eyes rolled back in her head.

"It is embedded. Take her away," Master Bentley said, leaving the thoughtfish to grow fat on the mind of Amelia Maybelove . . .

Mantra

I *am the master of my fate: I am the captain of my soul.*

For certain, this mantra is against the teachings of the Regulators. They have ordained that all situations should be ordered, all people confined to certain roles and responsibilities, as dictated by The Book of Rules which is wielded so forcefully against us lesser folk. What need have Regulators of weapons, when they have that?

Many yearn to break free of The Rules; they meet in dark, secret places. Places where imagination, creativity, innovation, and the freedom simply "to be" are encouraged and enabled, instead of being stifled and kept for only an elite few to experience.

I am the master of my fate: I am the captain of my soul.

Such is the mantra, spoken quietly in hope during clandestine gatherings, where a lowly clerk of numbers can become a musician. A rough-handed farmer in burlap can become a tailor of silk or satin.

An under-aged whore become a student—because I was both of them, once.

I am the master of my fate: I am the captain of my soul.

Such was the mantra, whispered in desperation when discovery put paid to my active resistance against the Regulators and squashed flat any dreams I had of living a different life. This mantra is all I have left now of my defiance, and I cling to it as fiercely as a drowning woman would cling to a broken plank.

I am the master of my fate: I am the captain of my soul.

I will speak these words aloud when they lead me to the stake to burn me on a pyre of my own making. As the paper on which the words I crafted into forbidden stories of love and hope is used to fuel the flames around my feet, I will scream these words until the smoke rips my voice from my throat, my tongue is blackened and my flesh cooked.

But before that . . . I will write them for the last time. Here. Now. In my final hour, on a stolen scrap of parchment, in the hope that it will be read after I am gone.

Reader, break free of The Rules and the Regulators! Discover what your heart yearns to truly be—and live! Take up the mantra for your own.

You are the master of *your* fate: *you* are the captain of *your* soul.

Not the Regulators.

The Colour of Life

I am weighed down by the knowledge that I cannot leave this poky little shop. At least, not until I have purchased what I need to make the mourning blanket.

It's such a strange tradition—stitching the life of someone who's dead. When this one is finished, it will not hang on the wall as tradition demands. Not yet. Instead, it will lie across our half-empty marital bed . . . at least until the rawness of my pain eases.

I drift towards a rack of threads and reach out, towards widow's black, gravestone grey, coffin brown. These will best reflect my desolation—I cannot bear to consider any others. The greens are too alive, the red like pulsing blood, the yellow as blinding as sunlight.

"Can I help?"

I snatch back my hand, startled. There's movement in the darkness, somewhere between the multicoloured bolts of cloth and the cutting table; an old woman, rising from a chair. Her face is nut-brown and etched with a million creases and wrinkles—the language of life. How many of them, I wonder, were caused by laughter? And how many by tears, like mine?

She shuffles closer, peering into my face. Her eyes are a startling blue, bright and alert; they examine me. Suddenly they widen.

"Ahhhh. My dear child," she murmurs. "Come . . ."

Blinded by tears, when I had believed my eyes wrung dry after so many days of weeping, I am led to the vacated chair and pushed gently into it. A cup is thrust into my hand and I sip—something warm and sweet and tasting of summer. If only it could thaw the frozen waste which surrounds my heart.

While I compose myself, a length of three spans is cut from a roll of beige linen and spread out on the table. It is a blank canvas, which must be filled with the cold hard facts of death. My eyes seek out the dull threads on their rack and a shiver runs through me; they will look like tombstones when they are laid out in rows upon the fabric.

"Tell me . . ." the woman whispers. "Tell me all about him . . ."

My mind turns back time, dredging precious memories from the places I had hidden them. Words fall from my tongue, tripping over themselves in their haste to be heard.

"He was tall, strong, with hair the colour of sun-ripened corn and eyes like sapphires. We met at the festival, my scarf snagged on his waistcoat buttons because the crowds pressed us so close . . . The hill where he built our home was full of blooming heather when he carried me over the threshold . . . We toasted the first apple harvest with a bitter red wine . . ."

I leave out nothing. I tell her everything—about our Jacob sheep . . . the china doll he bought because it looked like me . . . how we used to watch clouds gather over the mountains and laugh when the storm broke over us. About the scented rose he planted when I told him . . . I told him . . . The words wrap themselves into a knot in my throat and refuse to be spoken. I swallow them down, describing instead the waving grasses in our meadows . . . the tiny butterflies we used to chase . . . the moistness of his lips when he kissed me . . . the glow I felt in his embrace . . . Temporarily, the one who now lies so cold and still is brought back to life.

Eventually I fall silent, drained of memory and exhausted by emotion.

"Look . . ."

Is it my lost love who urges so quietly, from beyond the veil that separates us?

"Look . . . see?"

No. It is just the shop woman, pointing. I follow the line of her finger.

Did I expect to see on the cloth the colours of visible grief—of a life lost? Then I am disappointed, for lying there is the full rainbow—of a life well lived.

My fingers dance across the spectrum of threads, for our story has been retold in riotous colour. Gone are the widow's weeds, the stone marker, the plain coffin. They are replaced with his blue eyes . . . the purple heather . . . the orange scarf . . . the brown and cream sheep . . . too many more to list. I devour all of them greedily with my gaze, touching and testing with my fingers, knowing every single shade to be representative of our too-short time together.

A frown puckers my brow when I notice the single skein of pure gold thread; I can think of nothing of which I spoke that it could represent. I look askance at the old woman.

She is smiling a secret smile. "For the future," she tells me.

The new life growing within me stirs. As I place a protective hand on my belly, I realise suddenly that the colour of life is only momentarily dimmed and marred by darker shades.

Soon . . . soon, all will be bright again.

Red Moon Rising

Then . . .

"A blood moon," Old Maud muttered into her near-empty glass.

"You what?"

She jerked her head up. "Blood moon!"

"Steady on, Maud. No need to shout. You'll make folk spill their drinks."

Maud tried to focus on the speaker. Damn her clouded eyes. Used to be able to see so much better . . . when she was young. She blinked hard.

Stefan's face swam into view. He was frowning at her. "What you on about?"

"The moon. It's a red one tonight. As red as blood. Means there'll be a beast born." Maud waved a hand vaguely in the direction of the door, narrowly avoiding Fat John's glass.

"Oi!"

Maud grunted an apology and pushed her glass across the bar. "'Nother one in there."

Stefan shook his head but obliged anyway. If Maud was willing to pay, who was he to say when she'd had enough? He set the fresh beer in front of her and leaned over the counter as she took a deep pull. "It's called a *harvest* moon, Maud. Happens every so many generations when the moon colours up on Brightest Night, so I've heard tell." He rubbed his chin thoughtfully. "Never heard it called a blood moon though."

Maud wagged a finger at him. "Well, that's cos you don't keep the old ways." She spun round at the sound of a snort. "Nor do you, Fat John."

"I'm too young for the old ways, Maudie. You do know, don't you, that when you're kicking up daisies, the old ways'll completely disappear?"

Maud set her glass down with a bang. "And what you goin' to do when I'm not around to give you the warning, eh, John? The old ways tell that a blood moon spawns a blood beast. Don't you roll those eyes and grin at me. I'm telling you true. I were a slip of a lass the last time we had one."

"Tell us about it," Stefan said.

Fat John laughed. "Aye, and we'll look out for beasties when we roll home."

Maud took a deep breath. Maybe some of 'em would listen, take heed . . .

"You ain't old enough, either of you, to remember the Dawsetts. Used to have a smallholding, up near Big Oak, they did. There were Ma and Pa Dawsett and five daughters. The youngest, Amira . . ." Maud paused, nodding at the memory. "She were my friend. I used to go up there regular. But then there were a blood moon . . . At the first sight of it rising, my own Ma shut us up so tight in the house, we couldn't find a chink to peep out of. The red moon was the bringer of the blood beast, she said. I thought she meant a bear or wolf, 'til I went up to the Dawsett's next morning . . ."

Oh, Eva, Maud couldn't bear the remembering. She snatched up her glass and downed the contents in one go.

"Whoa, steady on!"

The glass rattled against the bar as Maud set it down. "I saw Pa Dawsett first, throat torn open. The rest of 'em . . ." A shudder ran through her body, nearly shaking her off her stool. "All dead. Ain't never forgot."

The image was imprinted on her memory; torn flesh. Flashes of white bone in red meat. Blue-grey smears on the walls.

Stefan whistled and glanced at the clock. "Sounds nasty."

"Aye."

"Huh." Fat John turned away. "Nasty, but like as not some or'nary beast or other, mad with hunger."

"Twas a blood beast, I tell you—"

The clang of the closing bell cut Maud off.

"Time, gentlefolk please," Stefan called. "See your drinks off and away to your beds! You too, Maud."

The world was tinged with red when Maud stepped outside, but she kept her eyes on her boots all the way home. "I ain't goin' to look at you, Mr Moon, but Eva help them as do," she muttered.

Stefan had not long fallen asleep when the banging woke him up. He hauled himself to the window and flung it open. "We're shut!"

"Help!"

The voice, shrill with fear, spurred Stefan into action. He pounded downstairs, shot back the bolts, and hauled the door open. A girl staggered in, thrusting a red-blanketed bundle at him.

"Help her, please."

"Tanil?" Stefan snatched the bundle up, but didn't understand until the blanket, wet to the touch, fell open.

A hand fell free. A tiny hand; a hand connected to an arm that ended in a mess of shredded pink and wet redness and blue coils. He flung it away with a yell.

The girl threw her head back and screamed.

"Sweet Eva, protect us," Stefan whispered. He grabbed the girl and held her tight against his chest, smothering the screams, staring at the gory mess lying exposed on his floor. "There's nothing to be done, Tanil. Come, come away. Hush, child, hush . . ."

Now . . .

All I actually remember of that night is the red moon. How it rose and painted the world with ruby instead of silver and black . . . Everything else between the moment I stood looking at it and the moment I woke in a bed in the inn, is a black hole.

What I know, Stefan told me. Ma and Da and Ralph were still at the cottage. At least, that's who the bodies were assumed to be. There wasn't a funeral. Stefan took the baby back to be with them, and the whole lot was torched. Nothing left but charred stones and timbers.

Maud keeps muttering about a blood beast. Some folk, even if they believe in such a critter, think I had a lucky escape from the . . . thing . . . that attacked. But when Maud's in her cups, she tells anyone who'll listen it were me that slashed and tore my family to pieces, and she makes the sign against evil and won't let me serve her. Stefan won't have that, though. Tells her a slip of a girl couldn't have done what he saw done, and he'd never have opened his home to a murderer.

Maud ain't convinced. And there are more folks listening to her than to Stefan.

I take the slops out, and she'll be there, in the yard, watching as I empty the bucket. Stefan sends me on an errand and she's hobbling along behind me as fast as she's able, keeping me in her sights. Even when I've thrown the slops at her, or taken the long way round to where I need to go sometimes, she don't give up or bugger off.

Stefan laughed when I told him what I did, said Maud getting her feet soaked with old beer served her right. But then he got serious, said she's a good customer, that I must be respectful or he'll lose her business.

I try, but it's hard.

Especially now she stinks from what she calls her "protection." It's some concoction she's brewed up. Carries it with her in a tiny glass bottle. Dabs it behind her ears and on her wrists, like perfume. Not sure what she puts in it, but sweet Eva, it's not rose petals.

I've just set a steak pie in front of her, and even the smell of that can't overpower the stench rising off her.

"Enjoy," I say, and smile. But my nose wrinkles and Maud frowns at me.

I know she's watching me as I walk back to the bar. She's not the only one; three people make an obvious sign against evil as I pass by, but I bet more are doing it under the tables, so Stefan don't see.

"I'm going outside for a minute, clear my head," I say to him. "Maud stinks worse than ever tonight."

Stefan nods and grimaces. "Aye, I can smell her from here. Go on, I'll yell if I need you."

Fresh air. I stand in the yard and gulp down great lungfuls of the stuff until I can't smell Maud anymore. Then I sit on an empty barrel and look up, into the ink-black sky. The moon looks like one of the clipped coins Stefan's warned me to look out for when there's strangers in, but it won't be many nights before it fills out, becomes a fullweight silver penny on Brightest Night, thirteen weeks after the last one.

I don't want it to be Brightest Night. Last time, when the moon came up red instead of silver, *It* happened. And it's going to happen again. As the moon's gone through its cycle, passed through Blackest Night and fattened up again, what was a black hole in my memory has vomited up flashes of sight and sound and sensation from *that* night. I remember the blood beast. I remember how it roared and tore and ripped.

And I know where it's hiding, sleeping until Brightest Night . . .

I don't want to know. I don't want it to happen again. I keep telling myself it won't. Been praying to Eva that it'll be cloudy and the moon'll be hidden so it won't wake the beast. That everyone will stay away . . .

But why would they, a voice whispers in my head. Folks love a drink or two and a good gossip. Why would they decide to miss that?

I glance up at the moon again, and suddenly there's an idea in my head. Thank Eva, she's answered my prayers. Stefan musn't know—he'll not thank me for turning away custom. But perhaps, if I look sad over the next few days and tell a few folk, the sympathetic ones, that I wish

I could spend a quiet evening remembering my poor family on this first mooniversary, it might keep a few away, keep them safe and—

I smell her before I see her.

"Talking to the moon, girl?" Maud shuffles out of the shadows.

"No. I needed a piss. Mind where you walk."

She grunts and steps closer and I gag on her stench. What in Eva's name is she putting in that potion of hers to make it so foul? "Nice perfume."

"Keeps the beast away." She peers into my face, though I know she don't see too well. "I'm watching you," she whispers, and hobbles off into the night.

I t worked. Better than I could've hoped for.

"Where is everyone?" Stefan scratches his head. "Brightest Night's usually dead busy. But we've only got Maud and Fat John in, and it's only a few minutes 'til moonrise. Can't understand it, can you?"

"No," I lie.

He gives me a look. "Hmm. You alright, Tanil? You look like you've got something on your mind."

I lie again. "I'm fine." Except I'm not. There are no clouds tonight, nothing to stop the full moon from being seen by everyone. Including the beast.

Stefan's talking again.

"—guess it's to be expected, after last Brightest Night. You're bound to be thinking on it—" He stops then, glances at me from the corner of his eye. "Least said about that the better. Best for those memories not to get stirred up again."

Oh, if only he knew. The memories have already stirred, and soon, the beast will, too . . .

"Let's have a drink, eh, Tanil? Apple brandy. On the house for you two," he calls over to Maud and John.

Apple brandy? The beast won't want that. He'll want something completely different. Something warm . . . thick . . . metallic.

I catch myself licking my lips and tell myself it's the brandy I'm looking forward to. A tremor runs through me. Someone's walked over my grave, isn't that what folks say when that happens?

Stefan's loaded a tray with glasses and the brandy bottle, is taking them over to Maud and John.

I don't follow. There's a faint buzzing in my head, a pressure in my ribcage, and I move towards the door. Fresh air, that's what I need. Maud's smell's got to me again . . .

Who am I kidding? When I open the door, there, on the horizon, is a glowing sliver of silver which has drawn me to it, a sliver which grows and rises while the buzzing in my head gets louder until it's the only thing I can hear and I think my heart will shatter my ribcage with its pounding and I want it to stop so much—

The full moon springs loose from the earth and bounces up, into the sky.

And that's when it happens.

There's no gentle slide from me to it; the beast is just suddenly present, inside me, its senses alert, its whole being filled with the desire to feed. From somewhere behind my own eyes, I watch it flex my hands, note the muscles rippling under my skin.

We both hear Stefan telling us the brandy's poured and to shut the door, 'cause it's freezing with it open.

The moon is lending the beast strength and power. For the second time I'm powerless, locked in a body I no longer control, with no way out again until it's over.

I—It—we—push the door shut. And then we turn the key in the lock. Quietly, carefully, with only the slightest of clicks to indicate what we have done.

Then we walk over to the table where the three of them sit, and it shares with me the excitement caused by the knowledge that there is blood rushing through soon-to-be-emptied veins. It lets me feel in every fibre of the body it has taken over the tha-dump of beating hearts, soon to be torn from their bony protection. I try to scream a warning, but it is the beast who speaks.

"I know where the blood beast is," it says, quietly.

Maud looks at me; her bottom lip quivers. She knows, too. Has always known. The beast pulls my face into a smile as she fumbles with her potion bottle and tries to pull the cork. Even opened, it won't offer the protection she was hoping for.

"You what?" Fat John says.

"I know where the blood beast is," it repeats, and holds out my hand. All four of us watch the nails darken and lengthen into knife-edged talons.

"Oh, Sweet Eva—" Fat John's chair falls to the floor as he scrambles to escape. Except he won't. He can't. Pa and Ralph tried to when the beast attacked Ma and Anya, but I remember its impossible speed.

Stefan rises slowly to his feet, eyes wide. "Tanil?"

This time, the beast relinquishes my voice, but only for a breath.

"I know too," I tell Stefan, before me and the beast leap.

Keeping Up Appearances

I do my best to keep up appearances. And I think you noticed; you said your heart skipped a beat when you saw me at the bar.

When I saw you . . . mine didn't.

You see, the mechanical pump they implanted into my chest is guaranteed for fifty years. Tha-dum, tha-dum, every two seconds, for fifty years. The old organic one leaked like a sieve.

You like my hair? Yes, I'm currently a redhead, but who knows . . . this time next week, I could be brunette or blonde. I have a fantastic hairdresser who styles my wigs, because I have to disguise the metal plate in my skull somehow. There wasn't enough skin left to cover it, I'm afraid.

The unusual colour of my eyes . . . well, I was lucky, they matched the shade perfectly. The days of glass orbs are long gone; nowadays, they grow organic replacements. Imagine, hundreds of eyeballs, waiting in glass jars for victims like me. Thanks to modern technology, they can even mimic the movements of the remaining eye.

You compliment my dress, but think it strange to wear long sleeves in the height of summer. I have no choice. You really wouldn't like to see where my bionic arm joins the stump, even though the prosthetic is temperature regulated, covered in the latest flexi-skin, and capable of reacting to the few remaining nerves I have left to make it more realistic. And thank goodness for false nails . . . because the ones on my left hand will never grow again.

But if you looked at me, you'd never know. You can't see what he did to me.

Homeland

Councilman Tartris slammed his fist into his saddle. "We will not go into this wasteland! Look at it!"

Anna swept her gaze over the barren expanse which lay in front of them. Withered grass stretched as far as the eye could see; even as far as the strange, flat-topped mountain in the distance. "The heart leads me—and we must continue," she answered, with a calmness she was struggling to maintain.

"No. I have had enough. We've all had enough." Tartris shook his grizzled head and gripped the reins more tightly; Anna wondered, fleetingly, whether he wished it were her neck instead. "We began this futile search twenty years ago and are no nearer a homeland now, than we were at the start. The Council have decreed that the exodus stops, my lady," he growled. "Right here."

She had expected it—there had been rumbles of dissent for weeks as they drew nearer to the plains. But to finally hear it was more painful than she'd imagined. Tears prickled Anna's eyes, but she refused to let them fall—not in front of this pompous ass. "So you would betray the heart?"

Tartris laughed, a grim sound with no mirth in it. "Has it not already betrayed *us*, by leading us on a wild goose chase? The years have been filled with nothing but women's dreams and heartsickness. It is time we listened to reason and common sense instead. We go no further, my lady." With a click of his tongue, he turned the horse and galloped away, towards the tented city that had taken root where there was still grazing for the animals, wood for cooking fires, and water.

Anna stared, unseeing, at the acres of scorched grass swaying in the breeze. "I must continue," she whispered. "We are so close—I can feel it calling . . ."

"*I do* understand, my lady—but this is madness!"

Anna watched as Councilman Draygon paced the floor of her tent. He reminded her of the caged lions they'd seen beside the pools of Tramanth.

"The Council cannot forbid a priestess to continue searching," she told him. "I will take six of our best hunters and plenty of provisions and water in an ox-cart."

"And what if it's not enough? What will you do if you run out of water, or fall ill, or the wheel drops off the cart?" Draygon ran his fingers through his hair and sighed deeply. "Perhaps they were right about the heartsickness. It seems to affect every lady of the heart in the end."

Anna rose swiftly from her chair, two spots of livid colour on her cheeks. "Even *you* doubt me?" Her entire body quivered with suppressed rage.

"I didn't mean . . . my lady, you know I . . . bah!" Draygon clenched his fists and pressed them to his forehead. He took a deep breath, then let it out in a long sigh as he lowered and unclenched his hands. "Anna," he said softly, "we were both children when we began this journey. Your head—and plenty of others beside—was filled with the idea of discovering our ancient homeland. Spending aeons in captivity robbed us of our identity. Of course we long to rediscover who we are and where we came from! It's perfectly natural . . . but we do not need to spend even more years on a fruitless search to fulfil that dream. We can make *anywhere* our home now." He reached to take Anna's hand, but she snatched it away.

"It is a *dream* that our people have clung to for centuries," she snapped. "How do you explain the heart in all of this?"

Helpless in the face of her anger, Draygon shrugged.

"I will not give up on the heart. It is part of me, Councilman, part of who I am and what I represent, and we are *so* close. I can feel it, here." Anna pressed the first two fingers of her right hand against her heart and glared at him. "I *will* find our homeland, with or without your support. Or I will die trying."

Draygon watched Anna and her hunters as they crawled away across the scorched brown land. She had insisted on going, even though he had begged her to stay. At least he had managed to persuade the Council to allow her a single lunar cycle before the people began to retrace their journey in search of more hospitable surroundings. Determined for some reason to reach the mountain at least, Anna had been confident that she would be back well before then.

Draygon hoped she was right. Time was running out for Anna, in more ways than one.

It was a lookout who spotted their return, two days before the Council's deadline. Draygon leapt onto his horse and galloped out into the wasteland to meet the caravan.

"We found it!" Anna called, as he drew closer.

"What?"

"A great city . . . inside the mountain!" one of the hunters shouted.

"Inside the—"

"Aye! And the heart is everywhere!"

Draygon pulled alongside the ox-cart, where Anna sat beside the driver. "My lady of the heart, is it true?" he asked, suddenly in awe of his priestess and a little ashamed of having ever doubted her.

"Yes." Anna's eyes twinkled mischievously. She had never looked more radiant. "Do you want to be there when I tell Tartris?"

"My lady? It is time."

Anna remained by the window and gave no sign that she had heard Councilman Tartris. She could feel the impatience radiating from the rest of the Council, but decided to make them wait a little longer while she drank in the reality of their new world.

Deep within the dormant crater, a great city was rising from the ruins of one which was millennia older. Just three lunar cycles after the Great Descent, and already there were the green shoots of wheat and corn colouring the fertile inner slopes. The people and animals who had been dying of hunger were now full-stomached, and the new-built watermills were drawing fluid of such clarity into the wellpools, they rivalled the turquoise waters of Tra-manth.

Anna sighed as Tartris tried again.

"My lady of the heart . . . the people are waiting."

"Our people have waited for centuries already, Councilman. What are a few more minutes, when added to that greater measure of time?" As she turned towards them, every member of the Council bowed, placing the first two fingers of their right hands on their hearts as they did so.

"Rise." Anna's silver-grey gaze swept over them, resting for a moment longer on Draygon before moving on. "Our forefathers hoped and prayed for this moment. They waited lifetimes . . . and yet it is we who are to see the fulfilment of their dreams. Let us not forget what we owe to those who kept the faith before us." She took the arm that Draygon offered. "As you say, it is time."

As they walked along the corridor, trailing the rest of the Council in their wake, Draygon was intensely aware of Anna's cool hand, resting lightly in the crook of his arm. Today, she was very much his priestess. He glanced sideways at her.

Her hair had been brushed till it shone like copper, the thin silver band which represented her exalted position resting lightly on her brow. Like many, she had chosen to wear red today—the colour traditionally associated with the heart—and the fabric of her gown hung loose from her shoulders, hiding her form within its folds. Over the dress, she wore a sleeveless surcoat of white silk shot through with threads of silver, so that she appeared to shimmer in the torchlight.

"Do I have a smudge on my nose?" Anna asked quietly. "Only, you are staring so hard, I fear I must have applied the paint wrongly."

Draygon felt the heat rise in his cheeks. "No, my lady. I find the patterns strangely enthralling." He always had—the green swirls across her cheeks and around her eyes enhanced rather than marred her beauty.

A smile flickered across Anna's lips. "As did I, when I tried painting them the first time. Do you remember?"

"How could I forget? You insisted on practising on me!" Draygon chuckled.

They walked on through the crumbling temple in silence, each lost in their own thoughts.

When they finally emerged onto the balcony, high above the people, a roar rose to greet them. Draygon released Anna's hand, content to remain in the background with the Council while the priestess stepped forward to receive the adulation of her believers. The silver robe shone more brightly still in the light of the twin suns, and Anna dazzled all whose gaze fell upon her. She raised her arms, calling for quiet.

"Centuries ago," she called, her voice carrying over the masses and echoing back from the sides of the crater which completely surrounded them, "our people were enslaved and taken far from their ancestral homeland. Yet their heart remained strong, hidden from its captors and continually whispering to the priestesses of home. Over the years, memory faded until we were left with only the heart and our belief that there was somewhere in this world that was ours—that we could truly call our own. Since we left captivity, we have travelled many leagues; we have experienced hardship and seen many of our loved ones pass over, their souls now carried with us in our heart."

Anna's voice wavered as she recalled all whom she had reassured that they would find a home—soon. But it hadn't been soon enough, for some. She breathed deeply before continuing. "We have experienced the joy of marriage oaths and births and seen our children grow into adults. I, myself, was no more than a child when we began this journey, and I thank the heart that I have lived to see the rediscovery of our homeland—this is the place where our story began!" Tears sprang into Anna's eyes and she smiled through them.

"My people," she called, her voice rising high into the circle of blue sky above them all. "My people, we are home!"

Cirque de la vie

Roll up, roll up, to the greatest show on earth!

We sit next to each other in the theatre. Two single strangers, with a shared love for *Bat Out of Hell*. Chat during the interval as we eat our ice creams, and when the lights go up at the end of the performance, you say we ought to grab a drink together, talk the show over . . .

Riding bareback

One drink leads to another. And then back to your flat. And to making love to the sound of Meatloaf. Only one thing's missing, but you say you know when to pull out . . .

Clown

What a frickin' idiot I am. Two parallel blue lines. In a quest to fool the world, I paint a smile on my face while I wonder what to do next.

Trapeze

It's what I want. Honest. I'm still swinging between excitement for the future and gut-wrenching terror for the same thing twenty times a day, but I'm holding on.

Juggler

Work. Doctor. Work. Hospital. Scan. Work. Clinic. Blood test. Work. Ikea. Shopping. Work. Decorating. Clinic . . . How the hell am I supposed to get everything done to this deadline?

Elephant

A lumbering body I don't recognise any more. Thick ankles, swollen legs, and an expanding belly that stops me seeing my toes.

Human cannonball

"This one was keen to make an entrance. Shot out so fast, I needed my catcher's mitt!"

Ringmaster

And here you are. The controlling influence in this new world of ours. Small, perfectly formed, and with a pair of lungs to rival Meatloaf already. I'll introduce you to him someday.

The Six of Tears

On my fifth birthday, Da died.

On my sixth, Ma remarried. Which might've been a good thing, except the man she insisted I called Da from then on watched me far too much for my liking as I grew.

On the eve of my thirteenth birthday, he cornered me. Told me I was a woman, pretty much, and he'd help me make the full transition. A good kick in the nadgers was the answer to that particular offer, but when I told Ma what he'd tried to do, she didn't believe me. Turned straight to the cards.

Those seventeen cards had told Ma lots of things over the years. At first I couldn't understand how pictures of the Tears—the same sort as used to fall from my eyes whenever Ma landed a slap, or Da pinched me in a tender place—could tell her anything. My fascination with the suit grew almost as fast as I did; I watched and learned and laid them out when Ma wasn't looking, until I could see their answers for myself. Even when they gave *me* a different answer to the one Ma revealed when we'd asked an identical question . . .

That night, the eve of my thirteenth birthday, Ma drew three cards. "Has he done what she claims?"

Upright fourteen of Tears. Perverse.

Upright seventeen, the Tears so tightly packed together on it they were like a waterfall. Fickle.

Reverse six, the Tears falling impossibly upwards. Truth.

Yet she still called *me* the liar.

The next morning, I left. And I took Ma's Tears with me.

The fat little farmer's wife sitting opposite me shifts uneasily in her chair. "Are you certain?"

I lean forward and tap the table once beneath each of the cards I've turned up; the eight, five, and fifteen of Tears. All upright. "Unresolved issues, loss, and sadness," I tell her. I lean back with a sigh. She doesn't want to believe me. Is going to ask for a fourth, I know she is . . .

Sure enough, another coin clinks into the bowl.

"Lay a fourth."

Three is the usual number of cards consulted. Any less, and the picture often remains murky. More always costs extra, but the desperate and disbelieving seem happy to pay it, even if all it achieves is to confirm an answer that's already perfectly clear.

I nod, but take my time in the choosing. I usually wait just long enough to see the sweat bead on an upper lip, or a muscle to twitch uncontrollably . . .

Or in this case, for the farmer's wife to bite her lip so hard, it draws blood.

I flip a card over. Six Tears are falling towards the wife, and away from me.

"Truth," I say.

She deflates like a pricked balloon. She asked the question, and the cards have answered. There can be no doubt.

"I'm sorry, Goodwife Ramalkin. Your husband's debt has not been settled and you will lose the farm."

I was paid for my first readings in stolen fabric scraps—as well as in coin—by the girls who stitched fashionable gowns in the same dingy workshop where I found work sewing bone buttons onto plain calico shirts. Thank the gods I was at least enough of a seamstress to fashion from those same scraps a bag to protect my cards, and even to decorate it later with half a dozen silver Tears, the thread for the embroidery pulled from Ma Bakerley's shawl when she wasn't looking.

It was Ma Bakerley, though I didn't know her name at the time, who caught me in a reading and determined my future.

Sarai Nugent had wanted to know if her young man would ever make her respectable; I'd turned the first two cards—the ten and four, both upright, for love and success—and was reaching for a quite frankly unnecessary third, when Ma burst into the workroom, her new plum velvet skirt gaping at the side.

"Where is the girl who misread my size so abominably? The skirt is—" Her eyes narrowed when she saw us. "What's this?"

"Oh, mam, it's just a bit of fun," Sarai said quickly, shooting to her feet. "Conni plays at reading the Tears."

"Plays at them, does she?" Ma Bakerley dropped into the chair Sarai had so recently vacated and fixed her beady little eyes on me. "I like games. Tell me, my little card player, did the maker of this skirt measure wrong?"

Sarai had had her answer, so I turned the ten and four back over, gathered all the cards together and shuffled them. "Three cards, mam?"

Ma folded her arms. "Two."

Two. No room for error or ambiguity, then. Thank gods my hands remained steady as I laid all seventeen cards out again, for I was shaking inside. I would have to be very certain, because my gut told me the woman in front of me knew a thing or two about the Tears . . .

I am proud of my ability to read the Tears. There are no tells on my cards, for as soon as any hint of the base card shows through the carefully painted ink, I make sure to cover it with fresh. Even on the edges. I'll not be accused of orchestrating a reading, or reading false. Not after what my own ma used to do. *I* let the cards speak. They cry out to me in a way I cannot explain but always recognise.

The first called and I flipped it over sideways. Reverse five. Gain. The second took a little longer to make itself known, but eventually . . . Upright twelve. Fact. The meaning was clear.

"Well?" She had a calculating look on her face, did Ma Bakerley.

"The girl measured true, mam." I braced myself for what I knew would follow. "'Tis you who've changed . . . some gain in weight?"

Her face reddened 'til I thought she would burst with indignation. Instead, she burst out laughing.

"Well, well," she said eventually, wiping real tears from her eyes. "You're a brave one, and no mistake." She chuckled again and wagged a finger at me. "Come see me tonight. Eight of the clock, at the Pig's Head. You know it?"

I nodded.

"I could use a lass with your skill. You're wasted here."

I'm in my reading room, pouring a glass of cordial to slake my thirst, when slender arms snake around my waist and a body presses hard against my back.

"I've a question to ask," a soft voice purrs in my ear. "Will you read for me?"

I set the jug down as the heat of desire rises in me. "I don't need to." I spin within the confines of her arms and look upon her beloved face. "The answer to your question, Mirande, is forever the ten of Tears, upright."

We've played this game so many times, she and I. A pretty frown clouds her face for a moment as she pretends to think. "Ten? Hmmm . . . reward?"

I shake my head, and she brings her own closer.

"Gentleness? No—sensuality." Her lips brush mine.

A shock of lust jolts me to my core when her arms tighten around me, pulling me closer.

"Love," I whisper.

"Love," she breathes, and kisses me fully.

I am lost in the taste, the warmth, the smell, the touch of her, bereft when she breaks away too soon.

"You've had a good day?" She picks up the bowl and stirs the coins in it with a deceptively delicate hand.

"Not bad. What about you?"

"Full house tonight." She twirls, and the blue gauze of her dress floats out like a cloud around her. "There's a foreign duke in town. Heard about the Bluebird and wanted a private show, but Ma put him right. Told him he had to pay for a seat in the theatre like anyone else."

I nod, unsurprised. The Bluebird—my Mirande, an aerialist of some considerable talent—was added to the theatre bill just two weeks after Ma Bakerley added a "Reader of Tears" to the static circus she owned and ran. The Bluebird soon became the act that everyone wanted to see.

Including me.

But it was my basic sewing skills that brought us together on my sixteenth birthday, not a performance.

"The Bluebird's shed some feathers," Ma told me. "There's no one booked in for a reading of the Tears 'til ten, so get yourself down to the dressing rooms and stitch them back on before her show starts, will you?"

It wasn't easy, but I did it. I stitched those glorious blue plumes onto the seat of a sequinned leotard and was giving it a good shake to check their security when Mirande arrived to get dressed and made up.

I loved her from the first moment I saw her.
And before too long, she loved me, too.

On the first night the duke came, Ma gave him the best seat in the house and arranged "with great difficulty" a brief meeting with Mirande after the show.

"You should have seen him, so tall and handsome," my bluebird told me as she undressed later that evening. "Eyes as blue as my feathers, hair as black as your cards. He's coming again tomorrow."

Was I jealous? No. I'd seen it all before. There were always men, happy to watch Mirande swing and leap and twist above their heads in a parody of flight, who then declared undying love and promised her the world if only she would succumb to their charms. The Bluebird would laugh prettily and flutter her eyelashes in public, then come home to me.

I had no fear either, then.

The duke came to watch the Bluebird every day for two weeks and sent her a bouquet of exotic flowers after each performance.

Reverse nine. Generosity.

Mirande said the blooms made her sneeze and sent all of them on to the sickhouse for the patients to enjoy.

At the beginning of the third week, the duke sent a caged bird instead, a strangely exotic creature with a ruff of blue feathers, a tail three times the length of its body, and the sweetest song I ever heard. He also sent a note, assuring Mirande of the sincerity of his affections.

At the end of that week, she opened the cage door and let the bird fly out of the window.

Upright three. Confusion. Upright two. Disappointment.

His next gift was a dress, bejewelled and bedazzled in every shade of blue known to woman, and a promise that if Mirande would consent to be his odalisque, he would give her anything and everything her heart desired.

Mirande laughed. Said she didn't need anything, and the dress was far too heavy to be practical. She tossed it carelessly onto a chair in her dressing room, told me to unpick the jewels from the fabric, and sell them.

Upright thirteen. Anger. Reverse seventeen. Perseverance.

By the eve of my eighteenth birthday, I am getting worried. The Tears have shown a building picture and I try to warn Mirande after the show, tell her I'm convinced the duke will continue to woo her until she is entirely his.

"He will bore of me soon. They always do," she says.

"If he doesn't, tell him about us." I catch sight of my reflection in her mirror; I am frowning. "That should put him off."

"Never! You are my secret love," she says, seizing me and pulling me into her embrace. "I've told you, he's nothing to me. *You* are my world."

Her kiss is tender, and I melt into it until there is a knock on the door. I move swiftly away from her, busying myself with straightening all the powders and paints on the dressing table.

"Come in," Mirande calls.

I glance towards the door, which stands unlatched, and my blood freezes when it opens.

"My Lord!" Mirande sinks into a low curtsey.

I sink too, because my knees give way.

The duke—for who else could this man possibly be?—seems to fill the dressing room. He is exactly as Mirande described him; tall, dark, exceedingly handsome, with piercing blue eyes. Do I imagine them flicking in my direction?

"Bluebird," he says, bowing low. "Forgive my intrusion, but I have brought you what must of necessity become a parting gift." He offers her a blackwood box. "You have given me so much pleasure in recent weeks, I hope you will wear it sometimes and think of me?"

"You are leaving?" Mirande opens the box.

Gods, she should not have sounded so hopeful.

"A certain matter has come to my attention which means that tonight will be my last in the town. Alas, I will miss tomorrow's performance. Perhaps your . . . assistant . . . would like to take my seat instead?" He looks at me then and smiles a smile that does not reach his eyes.

"Oh, Conni never watches. Never has. She can't bear to see her Bluebird fly." Mirande snaps the box shut before I can see what's inside. "It's beautiful, my Lord. Thank you."

The next day, Mirande's birthday present is given to me in a blackwood box I have no trouble recognising.

"This is what *he* gave you." I can't keep the sharpness from my voice. She smiles. "I know, but he's gone now, and I want you to have it. You'll see why."

Inside the box, nestled on a bed of white velvet, is a necklace. Hanging from a delicate silver chain is an exquisitely enamelled bluebird in flight.

"You see?" The bluebird nestles at my throat when Mirande fastens the chain and plants a kiss at my nape. "Now I'll always be with you." She turns me to face her. "We'll celebrate your birthday properly when this show's done and I'm down, yes? I'll see you in an hour," she throws over her shoulder as she leaves.

I take a seat at the dressing table, stare at Mirande's gift in the mirror, and hear the muted roar of applause from the theatre. My Bluebird has stepped onto the stage.

Something unsettles me about the duke's abrupt departure. My gut roils, and acid taints my mouth. I must know . . .

I fumble in my pocket for the scrappy bag, pull the cards out, and ask my question over and over as I lay them out, faces down. Then I force myself to stillness, and wait for the Tears to speak . . .

Reverse ten. Love.

Upright four. Failure.

Upright fifteen. Sadness.

It's the same three I've seen time and again, whenever a new beau has tried unsuccessfully to woo my lover. No reason to expect the duke to feel any different. But the Tears have not answered the question I asked. Is it *really* the end of the duke's interest in Mirande? To a backdrop of orchestral music, accompanied by ooohs and aaahs from the theatregoers, I shuffle the cards impatiently and lay them afresh.

Upright six. Deception.

Reverse three. Clarity.

Reverse ten. Jealousy.

Does he know? About me and Mirande?

"There was no deceit," I tell myself desperately, my heart thudding uncomfortably against my ribs. "The duke assumed."

I have turned three cards. It should be enough, but it's not. The cards are continuing to call. I obey them and keep turning . . .

Upright thirteen. Anger.

Reverse seven. A clear path.

Upright eleven. Brutality.

What does this mean? The roar of the crowd breaks into my concentration, and I know my Bluebird must be flying high above her audience.

The cards are shouting at me now, insistent. I've never heard so many, can't turn them over quickly enough to satisfy them, my hands shake so badly. There are too many Tears in front of me, far too many Tears . . .

Reverse one. Victim.

Reverse four. Success.

Upright sixteen. Death.

"No . . . no!" Real tears drip onto the silver-inked ones on my cards, blurring their carefully drawn lines.

There is only one card left to turn, and it is screaming. I clap my hands over my ears, but am deafened still. It will scream until I flip it—

The screaming is not coming from the card. It is coming from the theatre.

In one terrible moment, I see everything in the flood of Tears laid out before me. The duke, standing at a dressing room door left carelessly ajar. His money changing hands. A rope sawn half-way through on the trapeze. A single feather, drifting slowly down from the roof.

The last card is the six of Tears, reversed.

Truth.

The Tears *always* provide answers.

Dreamer

Cassia set her goblet down untouched and took a deep breath. "I dreamt about you last night," she said. "You were in the sanctum." She lifted her head, watching for a reaction.

There was none. Alchek's attention appeared to have been entirely diverted by a platter of sweetmeats; only when he'd selected a delicate pink truffle did he respond and show that he had heard. "So, you dreamed I was in the place where the ability to read minds is endowed upon those deemed worthy. Hardly surprising, given what's happening tomorrow."

Alchek had been chosen to receive the gift of Reading a week ago. On the morrow, he would be installed to a position of authority that few could ever hope to reach. This gifted ability could be used at any point in the future within the law courts, in business transactions, in politico . . . and, saints protect her, within their marriage. Was that why she'd dreamt the same thing three nights running? And why, with each repeat, her sense of foreboding had deepened until she could keep silent no longer. Tonight was her last chance to persuade him not to accept the gift. She tried again.

"But the dream . . . It was just so . . ." She fell silent and turned away.

"So . . . what?"

Saints, she should've kept her mouth shut. A sharp note had crept into his voice.

"I am aware that you do not support me fully in this endeavour, Cassia. Saints know why. But tomorrow your husband *will* be a Reader."

And then, she would have no secrets. Ice ran down her spine.

"Until that time I am not blessed with the ability to read your thoughts—so I will resort to more usual methods of communication. Tell me of your dream."

"Mayhap I should keep it to myself. You'll only think it a ploy to keep you from your destiny."

"Ha! No woman's dream will keep me from my intended future."

"It might." She dared to look up at him. "What if the dream is in fact a nightmare?"

He waved her comment away. "I daresay I will be exposed to worse when I am able to plumb the depths of depravity which exists in some minds. There is no fact, no truth, in dreams. Now, tell me."

Cassia shut her eyes, hoping he'd think she was trying to recall the details. In reality, she couldn't bear to look upon the face she'd seen so changed in her dream. "You . . . were in the sanctum. Standing. In front of an altar."

"There isn't an altar in the sanctum."

"I know. But in the dream . . . there was. It was black as ebony. Stone. The Readers circled it, watching. Piled on the altar were thoughts. Strands of thought. Some short, some long, many somewhere between. Dark, light, glittering, dull. Like cords and ribbons . . . As sharp as razors, some of them. And I was suddenly afraid. *So* afraid. For you."

Her hands shook as hot tears leaked from under her lids and scalded her cheeks.

"Cassia, don't cry, please." His voice softened, misunderstanding. "You know it won't be easy for me to be a Reader. You always knew."

She opened her eyes and stared at the face swimming in front of her. "But in the dream . . ." She gulped, remembering the fear that had closed her throat and stolen her breath from her chest. "You alone stepped forward. You, and only you, picked up all those thoughts and turned from the altar . . . Gods help me, when you turned . . ." Her body was suddenly wracked with tremors.

Alchek grabbed her hand in a vice-like grip. "Cassia, calm yourself."

But she could not. Not now, not in the remembering. "They attached themselves to you, Alchek. The sharp thoughts, the dark ones. Wrapped themselves around your head. Sliced into your flesh, cutting and carving. I tried to pull them away, tore at them 'til my hands were bleeding—"

"It was a dream, Cassia, just a dream!"

"No! It was real. I felt the sting of their edges!" She tugged her hand free and turned her palms to him, so that he might see the criss-crossed tracery of fine scarlet lines. "I feel them still. But I couldn't save you. Your face . . ." She reached out then, as though to lay her hand against his cheek, but checked herself. "Your face. Turned into something bloody and monstrous . . ."

Alchek slammed his fist down on the table. "This is madness, Cassia. You had a dream. A bad one, for sure, but it was only a dream. I have spent years preparing for this moment, am fully aware of what is to come when I begin to Read. Reading the minds of men, seeing their darkest thoughts, will protect our people as it always has. It will not change me."

She had failed. "Are you sure, Alchek," she said softly. "Are you *really* sure? Because the thoughts you picked up, the ones that cut you so deeply . . . were all mine."

The Silent Princess

Once upon a time . . .

But which time, exactly? There are times of then, times of now, and times of yet to come . . .

And there are other times.

In such another time, when the ganderbuss trees were in blossom and the river rushed green from snowmelt, a sickly babe's incessant wailing sent her mother, the Queen, half-mad.

"How I wish the child was mute!" the Queen cried.

Which would have been as effective as a prample-juice poultice for a pimple, had not the western wind been blowing northwards that evening. And when *that* happens, wishes come true . . .

The baby was struck dumb.

Wracked with guilt, the Queen sought out the finest of fairies, the whitest of witches—and sometimes the blackest of them, too—to undo the damage.

On the princess's first birthday, the Hag of Hogart begged an audience with the Queen.

"She will speak only when she must," the Hag croaked. "The wish was made in desperation. Only in desperation can it be broken."

And so it seemed, as the princess grew. When she was hurt, she sobbed: silently. When happy, her body shook with laughter: silently. When angry, she stamped her foot and frowned, but could not give vent to her feelings with words.

The Queen whittled and worried about her child until the princess learned her letters.

With the learning came freedom of a sort; the pencil fair flew across the page, the previously unvoiced conversations pouring out onto paper.

Happy that—at last—her daughter could communicate, the Queen stopped searching for a way to break the bindings of her wish.

Until one autumn morn, when a waterfall of russet leaves was falling and the princess had reached her sixteenth silent year, a traveller arrived at the palace.

"My gift will make the princess speak," he told the Queen. "All I ask is for her hand in marriage when she does."

The Queen studied the young man with the long black beard and bright green eyes. He stood as much chance of succeeding as the others before him, which was none.

"Very well," she said.

And so the young man handed over his gift: a pen.

The princess took it up with a smile and wrote her thanks.

But what appeared on the page was not "*Thank you,*" but "*Buggity plopbasket.*"

The princess's eyes widened, and she tried again.

Plippetty stinkrabbit.

And again.

Noddlebum twiddletty.

And again and again, her scribbles filling pages and pages which she screwed up in frustration and cast aside. The mountain of discarded paper grew, covered in nonsense like *flackery muppetburger . . . Jubeelious mickettyflop . . . Pustulous creppittyho . . .*

The pen was bewitched.

But when the princess finally gave up and tried to throw it away—horror of horrors—the pen remained stuck fast to her hand. She pulled and pushed and tugged and twisted, but it would not come loose. Her only means of communication, snatched away. What cruelty was this, inflicted on her by the stranger?

Tears spilled from the princess's eyes; she stamped her feet and tore her hair, but the pen stayed where it was and the stranger waited, as silent as the princess.

In desperation the princess opened her mouth.

"Help. . . me," she whispered.

The bearded young man smiled and clapped his hands; the pen disappeared with a bang and a flash of green flame.

The wish was broken.

The princess had finally found her voice.

She married the bearded young man and if, sometimes, he wished for a moment's peace from her chatter thereafter, he never showed it.

Least of all when his wife whispered "I love you" in his ear.

Miss Aveline's Summerhouse

I know you must be tossin' up whether to buy that big ole house of Miss Josephine Aveline's now she's dead an' gone. For why else'd you be pokin' around in her garden? An' now, you found this.

There's somethin' you might like to know about this broke-down summerhouse . . .

But first, I gotta tell you I saw my Granny Elsie standin' at the foot of my bed when I were six year old.

Which wouldn't have bin so bad, but she'd been dead for two days and was laid out in our front room downstairs at the time.

That's why I believe in ghosts. An' that most o' the time, they make emselves seen for a reason. In Granny Elsie's case, it were so she could tell me I could have her brooch; the one with the glass-diamond spider sittin' in a silver-thread web. Momma tol' me not to be so stupid when I splained to her about it the next mornin', but I were proved right when they read Granny's will after the funeral. I hadn't learned my letters proper enough to read, so how come I know'd what Granny Elsie wanted me to have when she ain't never tol' nobody 'bout it 'cept the lawyer?

Course, I weren't allowed to wear the spider 'cept on high days and holidays, cos Momma didn't think it was right for a chil' to wear somethin' so precious ev'ryday. I'm certin she wanted that brooch for hersel' . . . but she weren't goin' to argue with the lawyer. Or Granny's ghost.

Anyways, I def'nitely seen a ghost an' so I believe in ghosts, but that don't mean I see 'em all the time. They on'y show 'emselves to me if they need to. Leastways, that's what I found. Like the time I seen three black an' white kittens sitting on the jetty, staring into the water. I kneeled beside 'em to look too, thinkin' I might see me a big fish. Instead, I see a sack, with three drowned kits inside when I hauled it out the water and opened it up. Lord, but Tyler got whupped good an' proper for that.

So don't get the idea I see dead people an' animals ev'rywhere. I don't. But when I do, it's important.

Which brings me back to this broke-down summerhouse you're standin' in.

See, I were sixteen when I picked up a live-in job, lookin' after Miss Josephine Aveline in that big ole house behind you. Most of the time, I din't see much of her. She kep' hersel' to hersel' in what she called the parlour while I dusted an' swept an' washed an' cooked for her.

'Cept for one day, soon after I started, I *do* see her. She's standin' in the hallway, starin' up at a big painting of an itty bitty house among some trees. She got lots of paintings, Miss A, and I like to look at 'em. I just never seen *her* lookin' at 'em before. So I sets down my bucket from where I washed the front steps, and stand beside her an' I say, I like that one.

She jumps like a startled rabbit. Do you? she says back. I painted it myself.

I look at the ole lady an' ask, You a painter, Miss Aveline? Cos I ain't never seen no brushes or paints in this house.

I was, she says, and points. That's the summerhouse in the garden, the last thing I painted before I put down my brushes. There wasn't the time you see, when Father needed me so much. She sounded sad. Will you excuse me . . . ?

Dory, I tell her. Old folks don't remember names so well. Especially if they rich enough to have people workin' for 'em.

An' off she goes to the parlour, her stick tap-tap-tapping as she goes, even tho' I don't think she really needs it to help her walk.

I stay a bit longer, takin' in the painting. An' as sure as I see you standin' before me now, I see a shadow in one of the windows of that itty bitty house Miss A painted. Nothing more than a smudge of grey where a smudge of grey don't look like it ought to be—an' which weren't there before, I swear. An' I get a coldness tricklin' down my spine, like I did when Tyler shoved snow down my neck.

I blink an' the smudge is gone. But it *were* there, an' I don' know what it means.

Next day, Miss A comes to find me. I need something from the attic, she tells me. You will have to go and get it.

O' course there ain't no way she can climb the ladder, so I go up and she stands at the bottom, hollerin' up at me.

A brown leather case, she yells. On the right, near the rocking horse. It will have the letters J-E-A on it.

Couldn't miss the horse. Nasty, ugly thing, with bulging eyes and teeth showin'. I seen real horses do that, when they about to kick or bite. Or both. An' sure enough, the case was right beside it.

J-E-A, I say as I'm comin' down the ladder with the case in my hand. Is that you, Miss Aveline?

She nods. Josephine Emily Aveline. Bring it to the dining room, will you? Put it on the table.

Well, she opens up the case and hauls out the biggest photograph album I ever seen, and she knocks her stick to the floor at the same time. I catches that stick before it can land and when my fingers close round it, I get such a pain in my head I think it's gonna burst.

Give me that, snaps Miss A, snatching the stick back. An' just like that, the pain's gone an' I'm left blinkin' like an idiot.

That's when I see, over Miss A's shoulder, another grey shadow. Big. An' person-shaped. An' I knows that time *exactly* what I'm seein'.

You got ghosts in this house, Miss Aveline? I blurt.

I don't believe in ghosts, she says. You may go.

But jus' before I walk out the door, I look back. An' that shadow? It's pointin'. Right at the table where Miss A's sat down, startin' to look at the pictures in the album . . .

Shadows and pain . . . Miss A and the album. They're connected, I'm certin of it. So later, when Miss A's dinner's cookin', I sneak back. I want to take a look at them pictures.

They're old. Most on 'em are shaded brown and cream, an' folks clothes are like what my Granny Elsie's granny wore when Granny Elsie were young. The gents have all got big whiskers and suits, while the ladies have hats and dresses down to the ground. There's writin' under some of the pictures, but it's too fancy and faded for me to make out much o' the words.

Then I turn a page an' see children. Two smilin' girls in flouncy dresses, big bows in their hair, standin' next to a man with whiskers so big, he could have birds nesting in 'em and not know. There's somethin' about the look o' these three that makes me think they're family. Underneath there's somethin' writ that I *can* work out.

J-E-A and M-A-A with Father.

So I know from the letters on the suitcase it has to be Miss A with her Pa. And as both girls got the same smile—perhaps they're sisters? The smile sits prettier on the sister.

I carry on looking through, seein' the sisters grow from girls to wimmin. Their Pa's in lots of the pictures with 'em, but he seems to be shrivellin' as time goes by until in one he's leanin' on a stick I'm certin is the same as the one Miss A uses. She's always standin' on his right side in the pictures, is Miss A, her smile getting thinner and thinner over time until it looks like she's suckin' lemons. And on her Pa's left, always the sister. So pretty, an' always beamin'.

About halfway through the album there's a photograph of the sister on her own, standin' right in the doorway of the house in Miss A's painting, then she ain't in the pictures no more. Just Miss A, with her Pa sittin' in one of them wheeled chair contraptions. Then Miss A, all alone . . .

I close the album an' go into the hallway. I stand lookin' up at the painting with the itty bitty house Miss A calls the summerhouse, an' I knows, deep in my belly, it's got somethin' to do with why M-A-A weren't in the album any more.

You seem fascinated by that picture, Miss A says, sneakin' up on me and makin' me jump.

An' right there an' then I decide to speak up. Miss Aveline, I say, there's somethin' about that summerhouse which needs tellin'. An' I think it has to do with your sister.

She freezes. With Marianne? she whispers.

Is that what she's called? I ask.

Miss A nods, real slow.

So I tell her I ain't mad, but I seen Granny Elsie and the kittens after they dead. And then I explains about the shadows I seen—the one in her painting and the big one in the dinin' room, pointin' at the photograph album. Miss A's eyes are fair bogglin' by then, so I don' mention her stick and the pain.

My sister loved the summerhouse, she tells me. She used to spend hours there when she needed a break from caring for our father. She's dead now.

Is that so? I think for a moment. Maybe she loved it so much, she couldn't bear to leave.

Miss A gave me such a look then. You think Marianne's ghost is here somewhere?

I shrug. Dunno for sure. I know I seen ghosts before, an' I think I might've seen one here, but I don' know if it's *her*. Would you like me to ask?

You can do that? Talk to a ghost?

I shrug agin. I talked to Granny Elsie, so it can't hurt to try, can it?

No. She gives me another strange look. Like she's workin' somethin' out. I am intrigued, she says. Shall we try the summerhouse first? As Marianne loved it there so much?

And off we go, into the garden. Thank the Lor' the ham hock wouldn't spoil for bein' longer in the cookin' . . .

The garden's overgrown, but Miss A leads the way through trees and bushes 'til we come to an open place. An' in the middle of it is the summerhouse.

It ain't what it used to be. Paint's all about peeled off, there ain't a pane o' glass that ain't cracked, an' I swear the roof's held together with a wish. But I knows what it used to look like from the painting, an' I can see why Miss Marianne must 'ave loved it so.

The door's so swole up, I need to give it a kick or two to get it open. Inside . . .

Inside, I see Miss Marianne. The smilin' sister.

Oh, Miss Aveline, I say. She's here.

But she ain't so pretty anymore. Her head is all stoved in, just like Tyler's was when he couldn't pay off his debt to Catfish Jerry.

Turns out I can def'nitely talk to ghosts. Miss Marianne tol' me everythin'.

How she and Miss Josephine grew up without a Ma, and how their Pa got sick and needed lookin' after. About how she met her young man, Edward, and how they wanted to get married, but that her Pa wouldn't let her. He told her she had to stay home, look after him alongside Miss Josephine. Miss Marianne weren't too pleased with that idea, so she planned to run away with Edward and marry him anyways.

Only problem was, Miss Josephine musta found out. And one evenin' time, when Miss Marianne had taken herself off to the summerhouse to hide her packed suitcase ready to run, Miss Josephine followed. Miss Josephine tol' Miss Marianne she had a duty to stay, and Miss Marianne got sassy, asked her sister why should she, when she had Edward ready an' waitin' to make an honest woman of her? And as there weren't a cat in hell's chance anyone'd ever ask Miss Josephine to marry, she may as well do all the carin' for their Pa on her own.

An' that's when Miss Josephine got real mad.

She grabbed their Pa's stick what had been left in the summerhouse, and she beat the life outta Miss Marianne, right before she dug her sister an' the suitcase into the dirt under this very buildin'.

Oh, you're leavin'—don't go! I ain't finished tellin' you how things turned out when I tol' Miss Josephine what Miss Marianne tol' me. Mind, I don't think you believe in ghosts. If you did, you'd'a seen Miss Marianne standin' by the window here.

And you'd'a seen me too.

Standin' right alongside her with my own head stoved in, cos Miss Josephine Emily Aveline din't want her summerhouse tellin' any tales.

Midsummer Madness

"Are ye well prepared?"

Aliz nods, her eyes wide and dark in her face. "I soaked the rope in rosemary water like ye said, an' the pegs were whittled fresh from holly."

"Good. And the other?"

"I have it."

No tremor in her voice. Will she remain as unaffected if she is forced to use it?

"Good." I tap my finger on my top lip and glance around the clearing. Have I missed anything? The symbol is marked on the ground in fine white flour, seven thick black candles stand at each of its points, the jug is filled with rosewater . . . "Let's get on, then."

Aliz sprinkles the rosewater, the scent of summer blooms hanging heavy in the air, almost masking the rancid stench of fear.

I lay myself down within the floured sign. Through my shirt, the earth feels warm. I keep silent as the still-damp ropes bite into my wrists and ankles, their aroma sharp and cutting against that of the roses. The ground vibrates under me as the pegs are hammered in and the other ends of the ropes secured.

Curtains of black hair frame her face when she leans over me.

"Is all secure?"

She nods.

"Ye will stay by me, and watch to see if the madness descends?"

"Aye, my love." She brushes my lips with her own.

"And if it does, ye will end me?"

Her eyes close then, shutting me out. But she nods. Again.

"Then move to yon trees and wait. Keep the blade near."

I turn my face away so I will not see her leave. So little time we've had, Aliz and I, but if the madness descends on me, as it does on some men on the Midsummer of their twenty-fifth year, she will at least have something to remember me by.

Pray hope the babe in her belly is a girl, for I would not wish this uncertainty on any son. And I doubt I have Aliz's strength to end a life if, by some miracle, I survive this night.

One Cold Coin

"Alma?" Tolya's whisper reaches me from the other bed. "I'm hungry."

My own stomach rumbles. "Me too. Stay there. I'll get the stove going and cook us some breakfast."

There's a thin layer of ice on the quilt; it shatters as I move and the cold cuts into my exposed skin sharper than any blade. Thank Sun I slept in my clothes, and that the stove didn't go out; it feels like the Lady came far too close last night.

She's picking us off, one by one. Being near to The Wall usually gives a bit more shelter than elsewhere in the shanties, that's why Ma took the room after Pa died. But with the Lady's current visit, The Wall may as well be paper for all the protection it's giving us.

At least we've woken this morning. Some won't have, and I'm not so daft I can't see what might happen if we're not careful. An icy draught catches the back of my neck and runs down my back. I shiver, and not just because I'm cold.

I don't bother clearing the ice from the window; there'll be nothing worth looking at even if I did, except The Wall. And that'll be just as grey and icy today as it was yesterday. And the day before, and the day before that. Instead I open the stove door, blow on the embers and coax them back to life.

Has it been one week—or two—since the coldfever struck Ma? I've been careful with the money, but there's barely any left. I tried, honest to the Sun, to make some, but my stitching's too bad; Ma's the expert.

When I tried to mend Arty's split seam for thruppence, I made it worse instead of better. And he refused to pay, the mean old goat.

Without looking, I reach for a log from the basket, but my fingers close around cold air. I glance down, can't believe what I see.

"What happened to the wood? Where is it?"

Tolya's head lifts a little from the pillow. "Ma was cold. I helped. Kept the fire going."

"Tolya!" My voice is too sharp, he ducks under the quilts and blankets. I close my eyes, bite back the rest of what I want to shout at him. No wonder the stove didn't go out. Not his fault though. He's too young, doesn't understand that every chunk of wood is precious. I'm a big girl, eleven next birthday, and Ma's shown me how to manage the draw on the stove so it burns the wood slow, not wasting any. I bet Tolya pushed too many logs in, opened the vents and watched the flames flicker and dance when there should have been a cherry red glow . . . How are we going to keep the Lady away now?

"Alm—" Before she can finish saying my name, Ma coughs, patterning the air with visible puffs of sick air.

I close the stove door quickly and move to the bed. I try not to notice the blue tinge in Ma's lips or her fever bright eyes. "It's alright. I need to go out for a bit, see Arty. I'll fry up the last of the sausages and a slice of bread or two when I get back."

"Tell . . ." She takes a steadying breath. "Tell him I'm better . . . I'll mend his coat. Tell him."

"I will," I say. But I won't. Arty made it quite plain he won't be coming to me—or Ma—for any mending ever again. I need to see Arty about something else.

Getting ready to go outside takes time. There are two coats to button up. A shawl to wrap over my head. A scarf to twist round my neck. Gloves to pull on. Boots to lace up. And then an old quilt, thrown over everything else, as a last layer of defence.

Tolya giggles. "You look like a walking wardrobe."

"At least I'll be a warm walking wardrobe. I'll be back, as soon as I can." I pick up our wood bag and the purse, then open the door just wide enough to squeeze out onto the landing. I shut the door quickly behind me, sealing Ma and Tolya and what little heat remains, inside. They say heat rises. It certainly feels that way; the temperature drops with every stair I walk down. I never thought four flights of stairs could be a blessing, but I was wrong. Our room, right at the top, is warmer than the ones at the bottom. I try not to think about my aching legs.

Outside, I suck in a breath; the shock of it burns my lungs. I fumble at the scarf, tug it up over my nose and mouth. I need to be careful. Last thing I need is coldfever, like Ma. Who'll look after her and Tolya if I get sick as well?

I hurry towards the market place, scattered ash and my hob nailed boots keeping me from too many slips; the Lady's applied a glasslike finish to the stones this morning. The sky opens out above the square, cloudless and silver bright. No cloud means no snow. Shame. It never feels quite as cold when it snows.

There aren't many sellers today, but I can see Arty's cart in the middle of a small crowd. And I can see the man himself, standing like a king atop his castle, on a pile of chopped wood in the back. I join the crowd, blowing on my fingers to keep them warm while listening to snatches of conversation as we all shuffle closer to what we're all hoping to buy.

". . . Old Ma Beckit, right by The Wall. Swore she'd seen the Lady's gown. Pater Grey must've seen it for sure. He was gone before dawn . . ."

". . . all five of 'em, in their sleep . . . !

". . . two families in one room, tryin' to save fuel. Only the youngest babby survived, cos he was closest to the stove. The other seven? Frozen solid. Every one of 'em."

Acid rises in my throat and my heart hammers against my ribs.

The Lady took so many, even those with fuel, in a single night? Then I must fill the woodbasket. With cold-clumsy fingers I pull out the purse. In it is a single coin, all we have left. A sixpence, but that'll buy enough wood to last two days. Providing that Tolya doesn't decide to help again . . .

"—can't help it if I ain't got much," Arty's yelling. "Ain't my fault if the Clerics bought a load more'n usual. This is all that's left."

"Damn the Clerics. They don't know what it is to suffer a visit from the Lady," someone shouts back. "Bet their woodbaskets are full. And yours."

Arty crosses his arms. "You want my wood, you pay for it."

"Two shilling, though! For a bag of logs that were only thruppence when I bought one last."

Two shillings? It can't be true, can it? I haven't got enough money, won't be able to keep the Lady away . . . The panic burns in my throat, and I swallow it down, trying to think. The words of a rhyme—"a bagful a day keeps the Lady away"—runs through my head. What do I do? I can't go back without wood.

"I run a business, not a charity," is Arty's response. "Wood's in short supply, so two shillings a bag. Take it or leave it."

There are a few with enough money to take it, but more without who have to leave. Some remain—friends or neighbours, pooling the contents of their purses, agreeing to split the bagful so many ways when they get it. Something's better than nothing after all.

I realise I still have one cold coin.

"I've got sixpence," I shout. "Will anyone split a bag with me?"

There's a man standing near the cart with a girl a bit older than me; his head shoots up. "Aye, I will."

I push my way through to him and he whispers something to the girl. She's nodding, watching me. The man holds out his hand, and I put my last sixpence into his gloved palm. Arty takes our money without comment, throws a few logs into the man's bag and passes it down to him.

I turn to the girl. "Shall we find somewhere to—"

Her shove sends me sprawling and she's off like a rabbit, the man slip-sliding behind her with the logs.

"My wood!" I scramble to my feet but already the thieves are out of sight. Tears of anger scald my cheeks, guilt burning even hotter inside me. The purse is empty. My woodbag is empty. I've failed.

The air's turned frigid, the wind biting. It knifes through all my layers, finds the chinks in seams, and draws the heat from my body as I drag my feet homewards. An open gate in The Wall catches my eye—or maybe it's the dark smudge of the forest beyond. Either way, I have an idea.

My nose is numb and my feet are points of pain at the end of my legs by the time I reach the forest's edge, but at least the rest of me's warmer from the walk. I've got no axe, no saw, but there'll be fallen branches, won't there? Perhaps pine cones too. I can fill my bag with them, keep the stove alight.

Except there's nothing here but the thinnest of twigs lying in the snow, covered in a frost that hasn't melted yet. I can't take those back. They'd take too much of our precious heat to dry them out before they offered up any warmth of their own.

I'll go deeper into the trees. There'll be more cover there, the wood will be drier . . .

There's a strange beauty in the forest. Icicles hang from bare branches, snow lies like a glittering carpet on the ground, and light plays between the trees in a silver-black-and-white world. But the cold sucks out any joy I might find in my surroundings as fast as it sucks away heat. The coldness is deep inside me now, making me shiver. I must hurry, find enough fuel to cook the sausages and keep us all from freezing . . .

Then I see it, like a scar in the snow. A fallen tree, rotten to the core, but with lots of thin, brittle branches poking out above the snow, just waiting to be snapped off the trunk. Numb hands make me fumble as I work. And then I start shaking so hard I can barely stand. Even my brain feels rattled. Why did I come all the way out here for wood? I could have gone home, broken up the chairs and table. Ma would have understood.

The light's fading. I've been out too long, must get back to Ma and Tolya.

I heave the strap of the bulging bag over my head. Which way is home? My teeth are chattering, my breath puffing from my lips in a shuddering stream of vapour when I push words out with it.

"F-f-f-footp-p-p-rints . . . wh-wh-wh-where are th-th-th-they?"

But the wind has scrubbed them from the snow, and there aren't any. Can't stay here. Must find the way, start walking.

One foot forward, then the other. Repeat. Again.

The whole world is ice and snow and trees. There's no colour except black and white. And it's cold. Bitterly cold . . . Freezing.

"T-t-t-tired." So tired. Need rest. Just for a moment, here, slumped against this tree.

Better. Much better. Not shivering now.

Someone . . . there, in the shadows. Tall and pale and . . .

The Lady is naked apart from icicles strung around her neck, her skin pale blue and translucent yet glittering, as though rimed with frost. Her voice crackles like ice when she speaks. "You dare to face the Lady of Ice?"

"Had to . . . Fuel . . . Kee y'away . . ." I'm mumbling. I try to push myself up with arms as heavy and cold as marble. Try to stand, but I can't feel my feet.

In one fluid movement she is beside me, staring. Her eyes . . . no colour. Except a circle of glacial blue around white irises.

"None can survive an encounter with me," she whispers.

"M-m-m-must. Ma . . . T-t-t-tolya . . . N-n-n-need to be w-w-w-with them."

She blinks. "You seek to be reunited? Allow me to assist." Leaning closer, she places a burning kiss on my cheek.

A rush of heat wells up inside me. Runs from my core along my veins, prickling my skin and making me sweat, warming even the tips of my frozen fingers and toes.

I'm saved! Must be—I'm burning from the inside out, warmer now than the time I sat too close to the stove and singed my skirt. I shake off the quilt, rip off the shawl and scarf. Still too hot . . . I tear at the rest of my clothes, stripping off the layers, until I am only in my shift. And *still* I am warm!

The Lady rises, watches, a hint of a smile playing at the corners of her blue-tinged lips.

The trees waver in a heat haze, and suddenly I am not in the forest. I'm home. The room's dark and cold, there's no ruddy glow from the stove.

But there's the bed, with Ma and Tolya fast asleep in it, unmoving. Heat radiates from my body and I laugh. I'll share this strange blessing of warmth from the Lady of Ice with them, warm them up too. To think we were so afraid of her, once . . .

The quilts lie smooth and colourless on the bed. I burrow deep into them, their feathery coolness soothing my raging skin. We didn't need the wood after all. We're together, all of us. And warm, thanks to the Lady . . . I'll tell them all about it, tomorrow . . .

My eyelids feel heavy. I think I'll go to sleep . . .

Circles of Stone

Tala had been given to the Guardians as an infant. She remembered nothing of it of course, being so young at the time . . . But as she grew, she'd seen others given in their turn and for a while had imagined herself in her own mother's arms, a bundle of baby-softness and plump limbs, wrapped perhaps in deerskin, or soft sheep wool, offered—freely or reluctantly? She would never know—to the protectors of the world.

And at these times, there was a rock, taken from the cairn and placed in the outermost of the five circles which surrounded it, to mark the Giving of a new Guardian.

Which was *her* rock, the one laid down by her mother? Tala had often wondered . . .

Not that it mattered now, so close to the end.

It was symbolic, she'd been told. It didn't matter which particular rock was *hers*, only that there was one, which moved at intervals to mark the stages in her life.

The first time "her" rock had moved was with the coming of blood; one stone, transferred to the second ring, just that little bit closer to the central cairn. A single step, part of the process of becoming a Guardian.

In Tala's seventeenth summer the rock was lifted and placed in the third circle as she was priested. She sighed, recalling the blazing sunrise of that morning, her bare skin dew-kissed where she lay prostrate in the grassy valley between The Mother and The Daughter rocks which stood sentinel over the gateway to The Circles. Admitted, at last, to the sacred ceremonies which kept the world turning, celebrated the seasons, and protected those who lived outside the Valley of the Guardians.

The move to the fourth circle came when she was given a daughter of her own to care for and educate; another woman's child given to the Guardians, to whom Tala was joined in virgin motherhood. And she had dutifully watched Eva grow, witnessed *her* first blood, and celebrated at *her* priesting. She could still remember the pride which filled her up at sunrise on that morning, when Eva had lain in the place where every Guardian had lain throughout the centuries.

The fifth move had been long in coming, and was by far the saddest. Thanks to her shrivelled womb, Tala had been forced to move her rock to the innermost circle which represented Ceasing. With the move came the giving up of the ceremonies—ceremonies which up to then had been deeply woven into every aspect of her life, giving it meaning and purpose. Ceasing also meant diminished status, when Tala was reduced to becoming the servant of other Guardians, whose wombs continued to bleed.

From that day on, each new sunrise brought with it the knowledge that this day could be Tala's last.

And then, before she was ready for it, it was.

Today, her rock would move for the final time, from the innermost circle to the cairn in its centre.

She knew the knife would be sharp, her blood would run fast, and she would paint the hollow between Mother and Daughter with a bloody sunset all of her own making.

Her consolation, as she walked unsteadily to that most sacred of places for the last time, was that one day, "her" rock would move between the circles again, for it was always The Way. There would be a new life; a Giving, a Coming, a Priesting, a Mothering, a Ceasing, and an Ending, all marked by stone.

As it had been, thus it would always be; the Guardians made it so.

Thread

When Lord Baraat sent my sister home on a gilded litter, my first thought was that she had not been wearing red when I last saw her.

The second was that she was dead.

I stood frozen at the door, unable to comprehend what I was seeing. Her face . . . what in star's name had he done to her face? Strong hands caught me when my knees gave way.

"She lives."

I looked at the speaker. What had he said? She lived? How could anyone survive . . . that? I was drowning in the blue of the man's red-rimmed eyes and my own grief as I listened to the words tumbling from his lips.

"My captain is dead! Baraat forced her to watch the execution . . . then he . . ." The soldier's helpless gesture encompassed so much horror and loss, I could hardly bear it. His pain seemed as raw as my own.

I stretched out a hand towards what, only hours before, had been my beautiful twin. "Bring her in . . . For the love of life, bring her in."

The soldier did not tarry; he had no desire to witness a second death.

I stitched the ragged edges of Salome's skin together carefully, weeping as I did for all that she had lost that night—her flawless beauty, her lover, her livelihood. For who would watch a dancer, however accomplished, if she was covered in a cobweb of scars? While I sewed, her fevered ramblings helped to piece together the events which had led to such wanton ruin.

I had known all about Captain Rabah, of course; he had escorted us to the palace the very first time Lord Baraat had ordered our very exclusive and unique form of entertainment. We learnt our craft together, my sister and I. Baba knew that the novelty of a girl dancing with her reflection would earn him more than separating his twin daughters. I don't know what difference the overlord detected between us, but after that first dance, it was only ever Salome who was ordered to attend him in the future. Each time, as one of Baraat's trusted bodyguards, Rabah escorted her to and from the palace. I watched the two of them once, when they thought themselves unobserved; Rabah kissed every bruise that Baraat had given Salome. And she let him.

Lord Baraat discovered their love.

His revenge was to force Salome to watch Rabah die the death of a thousand cuts . . . and then, apply a hundred more. To her.

That was then.

Salome recovered, though she is still afraid to look in a mirror at the monster she believes she has become. Instead, she takes my face in her hands and gazes at me long and hard.

"You, Shakira, you are all the reflection I will ever need," she tells me.

I smile, trying to conceal the revulsion invoked by the closeness of her ravaged features.

The memory of Rabah continues to consume Salome. "My darling is murdered!" she wails. "I can do nothing for him now. I would bury his body, but I do not know where it is!"

I do—but I shall not share the knowledge with her. The head of the traitor Rabah adorns a spike on the palace roof, picked clean by the carrion crows perching beside it like evil guardians. The rest of his body was buried in a secret location by the men who called him "Captain."

"I must demonstrate our love," Salome mutters, pacing up and down and wringing her hands. Then suddenly, she stops dead. There is a strange light in her eyes; the intensity of it frightens me. "I shall sew a mourning blanket."

Relieved to see her animated at last, albeit for a task borne from death, I scour the markets for the materials she will need.

On my return, the linen is unwrapped first; it is as white as the snow which tops the mountains of Ga-zrael. Salome runs the gossamer-fine fabric through her hands and presses it against her scarred visage. The second parcel contains silks from Si-ang; into her lap tumbles a rainbow of skeins. These, she lays side-by-side on a table. She takes the gold needles from their small packet and tests them, every point required to draw a bead of red from her fingertip before she is satisfied and lays them aside. The equipment is assembled, but Salome folds her hands in her lap and looks straight at me.

"I cannot begin until Baraat is dead."

My smile slips and a chill takes hold, deep within the very core of me. "But . . . but . . . you have everything you need. It could take years before the overlord ascends to the heavens! Why in the name of all the stars would you wait so long to begin? Dear sister, pick up a needle, I beg you. Start with the turquoise thread. See, it is almost the colour of the pools of Tra-manth."

"I cannot begin until Baraat is dead," she repeats, and turns her face to the wall.

Not only will she not begin—Salome refuses to eat.

"I cannot begin until Baraat is dead" becomes her constant litany. She watches me when she says it—as though willing me to bring about his death. How can I? What can I, a mere dancer, do? There is no unprotected way into the palace, guards would wrest a weapon from me and Baraat's Taster would detect poison before it ever reached the overlord's lips. I have tried to keep Salome alive by tempting her appetite with tid-bits and delicacies, but to no avail; nought except water passes her lips. And while she waits for me to achieve the impossible, she fades. Life ebbs from her, like the colour of an aging shawl washed once too often.

I do not want to lose my twin.

And then, as though the stars are listening to my increasingly desperate prayers, there is a chance. The Supreme Minister is visiting our city and Baraat wants entertainment for him.

I send word that I will dance.

The air is oppressive as I approach the palace, weighing heavier on my skin than the silk cloak wrapped around my body. The sky has taken on a yellowish cast and clouds tower over the city, threatening at the ferocity of the coming storm.

The inspection at the gate is a pointless exercise; with the cloak removed, it is obvious that I have no weapons upon my person. Except, perhaps, those with which all women are blessed. Yet the gatemen insist, examining closely what I will be taking into the building. I stand like a statue under their lecherous scrutiny. Eventually, they tire of ogling and wave me through.

Inside, the palace is an oven. I follow a eunuch to an ante room where I complete the final preparations. My diaphanous skirt and jewelled bodice are white, as is the mask which covers my face. I add the seven veils, wrapping them around my head, layering them until my body is obscured. I have become a ghost, a spirit.

Perhaps, an avenging angel.

When it is time, I walk barefoot into the feasting hall. The marble floor is cold against my soles, a stark contrast to the sultry air. Through the open arched windows I can see the clouds, bruised black and purple. The rumble of distant thunder is audible, even above the sound of bawdy laughter. Around three sides of this enormous space are the guests, their bellies stuffed with delicacies and their veins thick with wine. In their midst, in the position of honour, Baraat and the Supreme Minister are reclining on a mountain of fat cushions.

My courage almost fails me. Can they detect intention from a rapid heartbeat or the trembling of limbs? Have they the means to read my mind and forestall what I hope to achieve? It is a relief when a hidden drum begins to beat time and an invisible singer adds a single, liquid note.

An expectant hush descends.

As it has been taught, my body reacts to the music, every fibre of it vibrating and resonating and responding intuitively. I begin to spiral, my hands twisting and turning at the wrists, high above my head. The first veil, black as a moonless night, covers my head and shoulders. My arms ripple outwards, creating an ever-changing silhouette as I continue to rotate. A cymbal crashes; it is my signal to lift the veil and let it slip from my fingers.

The next veil is darkest grey, wrapped like a nomad's turban around my head and face. I unwrap the ends but hold them across my cheeks, keeping hidden what lies beneath. When finally it floats to the floor, there is a murmur of disquiet—the men were not expecting the mask.

A shade lighter, though still grey, the subsequent layer is taken from across my throat. I stretch it across my body like wings. I become a bird . . . a butterfly . . . I take flight . . . and then abruptly, my wings are clipped and fall away.

The fourth veil is released from where it binds my breasts and now I can be seen: all feminine curves and exposed flesh. Knowing this, I begin to tantalise and tease my audience. Undulations ripple up my torso. With sinuous movements I flick the fabric out, towards the men. It touches the watchers briefly before I draw it back to myself. Eventually, I release it.

The storm is getting closer. A strong wind blows through the arches, lifting my hair and blowing discarded veils towards the observers. Snatched up by eager hands, the fragile trophies are raised high in triumph. As though responding to the imminence of the storm, the tempo of the music increases yet again. My breath comes faster and I taste salt on my lips as sweat breaks out on my skin.

The fifth veil is drawn from around my waist and trails behind as I spin, faster and faster, becoming a blur of dove grey and white silk and golden skin. I am one with the music as the material flies away on the hot breath of the desert storm.

Palest grey, the next layer is taken from my hips. They jerk from side to side in response to the loss, revealing taut thigh and calf muscles through slits in the fabric of my skirt. Then a shimmy sets the jewels on my bodice glittering, shooting shards of light over the faces of the watchers. I reach out to them, fingertips brushing outstretched hands in a promise that will never be fulfilled. Another shimmy and even this veil disappears.

The last, tied tight around my buttocks, is pure white and sheer as mist. I arch backwards, sweeping the floor with my unbound hair as I untie the knot underneath my belly. I lift the fabric high as the music swells and changes and touches the deepest core of me. I am ecstatic, lost within the crescendo of sound, I dance for Salome's life and her satisfaction and I can do no more.

I fall to the floor as though dead.

Lightning stabs the darkened hall, thunder crashes overhead and the storm breaks. The applause can barely be heard above the sound of the deluge. Yet there is one voice I can still hear perfectly.

"Exquisite! Come, come!"

The Supreme Minister is beckoning me and I obey his command. I sink onto the cushion beside him, flinching at the explosion which follows another flash of blinding light. He notices my discomfort and chuckles, setting his jowls quivering.

"What a performance," he breathes. "I am completely satisfied." His arousal is evident; he makes no attempt to hide it. A jewel-laden hand hovers over his crotch, then descends to adjust the position of his manhood. "Such satisfaction deserves reward, does it not, Baraat?"

I risk a glance towards my overlord. He is darkness itself. From the tip of his head to the soles of his feet, he is all black and deepest brown.

I glimpse white teeth through his beard when his eyes rake across my masked features. A smile or a snarl?

The Supreme Minister leans closer, until I can feel the heat radiating from him. His breath is warm and fetid against my ear, the smell of his sweat, acid, compared to the freshness of the rain. "Name your desire. I give you my word—you shall have it. What will it be? Silk?" Clammy fingers walk slowly from my wrist, up my arm and onto my shoulder.

I shake my head.

"Jewels?" The same fingers stroke the hollow of my throat and slide towards the swell of my breasts, where they flutter against my skin. "Land? Palaces? You have only to say . . . I will give you anything." His voice is hoarse with desire, his eyes wide with lust.

Again, I shake my head and force myself not to recoil. I am so close . . . I rest a hand on the minister's thigh, then slide it up his leg. He responds with a moan of pleasure.

"There is only one thing I desire from the Supreme Minister," I whisper.

"Name it, name it!"

I withdraw my hand. Slowly, I untie the threads holding the mask in place and let it drop into my lap. When I lift my head, I see shocked recognition in Baraat's eyes and am glad of it. Before he can speak, I make my request.

"I want the head of Baraat."

I cradle the parcel against my breast all the way home.

I hasten to Salome's room. She is sitting at the table, framed by the window, her fabric and threads still undisturbed. I fancy that her ghost would probably look just the same—sitting motionless at the same table, its skin pale and translucent, its hair blowing gently about a ruined face.

But Salome is not dead yet, and I have brought something to keep her alive.

"Dear sister . . . I have something for you."

Salome turns enormous brown eyes upon the red-stained parcel I place upon the table. She lifts one corner of the cloth, still sticky with blood, and throws it back, revealing what is inside. I avert my eyes.

I expected a reaction, of course. A scream maybe? At the very least, a gasp. Not a girlish giggle of delight.

"I can begin." She laughs. "Oh, Shakira, thank the stars, I can begin!" Her ravaged face twists into an approximation of a smile and she selects a needle. Her fingers dance lightly over the threads which have been waiting so long to be used.

Then they dance on.

Salome plucks a single long black hair from the severed head and threads her needle.

Katherine Hetzel has always loved the written word, but only started writing "properly" after giving up her job as a pharmaceutical microbiologist to be a stay-at-home mum. The silly songs and daft poems she wrote for her children grew into longer stories. They ended up on paper and then published. (*Granny Rainbow*, Panda Eyes, 2014, *More Granny Rainbow*, Panda Eyes, 2015) Her debut novel, *StarMark*, was published by Dragonfeather in June 2016 and her second stand-alone novel, *Kingstone*, in June 2017. The first book of *The Chronicles of Issraya* was published in 2019. She sees herself first and foremost as a children's author, passionate about getting kids reading, but she also enjoys writing short stories for adults and has been published in several anthologies. A member of the online writing community Den of Writers, Katherine operates under the name of Squidge and blogs at Squidge's Scribbles. She lives in the heart of the UK with Mr Squidge and two children.

Visit Katherine's blog:
https://www.katherinehetzel.com/